W.H.G. Kingston

Captain Mugford

© 2025, W.H.G. Kingston (domaine public)
Édition : BoD · Books on Demand, 31 avenue Saint-Rémy,
57600 Forbach, bod@bod.fr
Impression : Libri Plureos GmbH, Friedensallee 273,
22763 Hamburg (Allemagne)
ISBN : 978-2-3225-7106-2
Dépôt légal : Avril 2025

Captain Mugford

By
W.H.G. Kingston

CAPTAIN MUGFORD

Chapter One.
Introductory.

We belong to a Cornish family of the greatest respectability and high antiquity —so say the county records, in which we have every reason to place the most unbounded confidence. The Tregellins have possessed the same estate for I do not know exactly how long; only I suppose it must have been some time after Noah disembarked from the ark, and, at all events, for a very long time. The estate of which I speak was in a wild part of the country, and not at that time very productive; but I believe that my father would not have parted with it for ten times its market value. It contained between four and five hundred acres of hill and dale, and rock and copse, and wood; its chief feature a lofty cape, which ran out for a considerable distance into the sea. On one side it was exposed to the almost unbroken sweep of the Atlantic Ocean; on the other it was washed by the tranquil waters of a deep bay, which formed a safe and picturesque harbour for numerous small craft which frequently took shelter there from press of weather when running up channel.

That headland, where the happiest half-year of all my boyhood's days was passed, is now dotted with several pleasant summer residences; its acres are marked off by fences and walls, and variegated with the diverse crops of well-tilled fields, and on its bay-side are occasional small wharves for pleasure-boats. Fifty years ago it was very different, and, (though, perhaps, I may be an old fogey and have that grey-hair fashion of thinking, with an expressive shrug, "Ah, things are not as they were when I was a boy!") I must say, far more beautiful to my eyes than it is now. You have seen a bold, handsome-bearded, athletic sailor-fellow, with a manner combining the sunniness of calms, the dash of storms, and the romance of many strange lands about him. Now, if our admired hero should abandon his adventurous profession, and settle down quietly into the civilised career of an innkeeper, or village constable, or shopman, or sedate church clerk, and we chanced to meet him years after his "life on the ocean wave," it would probably be to find a sober-faced gentleman, with forehead a little bald, with somewhat of a paunch, with sturdy legs and gaiters, perhaps with a stiff stock and dignified white collar—altogether a very respectable, useful citizen. But the eye and the heart could not find in our excellent acquaintance the fascination which so charmed us in our friend the brave sailor. So with our cape: fifty years ago, in all its natural wildness; in the beauty of its lonely beaches strewn with pieces of shivered waterlogged spars and great rusty remnants of ship-knees and keels; in the melancholy of those strips of short brown heath on the seaside, disappearing in the white sand; in the frowning outlines of the determined rocks that like fortresses defied their enemy the ocean; in the roll of crisp pasturage that in unbroken swells covered the long backbone of the cape; in the few giant old trees, and, more than all, in its character of freedom, loneliness, and isolation, there was a savage charm and dignity that the thrift and cultivation, the usefulness and comfort of civilisation's beauty can never equal.

My first sight of the old cape was when I was about nine years of age. My father took me with him in a chaise from Bristol—two days' journey in those times; and I do not think now that my year's tour of Europe, fifteen years after, was half as full of incident and delight as that my first expedition of a few hours. I can recall how the man at the toll-gate hobbled to us on his crutch; how my father chatted with him for a few moments; how, as we drove off, the man straightened himself on his crutch and touched the brim of his hat with the back of his hand. How well I remember the amazement with which I then heard my father say, "Robert, that man lost his leg while fighting under the great Duke in the Peninsula." I thrust my head far out of the chaise to look well at my first live hero. That sight was romance enough for an hour. Then the first glimpse of the top of the high cape, and my father's telling me that where I saw the haze beyond was the ocean, were sources of further reverie and mystery, dispelled, however, very suddenly when directly afterwards a wheel came off the chaise and pitched me into the road, with my father's small valise on my stomach. I remember the walk to the nearest house, which happened to be an inn, and how my father took off a large tumbler of ale, and gave me some biscuits and a glass of water. It occurred to me, I recollect, whether, when I became a man, I should be able to drink a full glass of ale and not be a drunkard, and whether my son would take biscuits and water and I not be conscious that he wanted to taste the ale. A thousand things more I remember—mere trifles in reality, but abounding in great interest to me on my first journey, which really then seemed of as much importance as Captain Cook's voyage around the world or Mungo Park's travels in Africa. It was a delightful day, the most interesting chapter in my life up to that time—brimful of novelty, thought, and excitement—but I shall not write its events in detail. What I have already mentioned will do as a sample. Late in the afternoon—it was the afternoon of a September day, the first fine one after a three days' storm—we reached the cape, just as the short sombre twilight of an autumn day settled down on land and sea. As the horse trudged laboriously along through the heavy piece of sand connecting the cape and the mainland, I was almost terrified by the great sound of waves, whose spray tossed up in vast spouts from every rocky head before us. The rush of waters, the rumbling of great stones receding with the current, the booming as of ships' broadsides—all these united to awe a little boy making his first acquaintance with the ocean.

When we drove up to the house, which was the only habitation on the point, not a light was to be seen, and the dark stone walls were blacker than the night that had settled down so quickly on the land. My father said there was no use to knock, for that old Juno lived in the back part of the house and was too deaf to hear us. So he led the horse round, and we went to the back windows. Through them we saw our old black castellan nodding, pipe in mouth, over the fireplace. She had not heard the noise of our wheels, and it required a vigorous pounding on the heavy back-door before old Juno, in much trembling, opened it to us.

"Oh my, Massa Tregellins, is dat you dis dark night! And Clump, de ole nigger, gone to willage. Lor, massa, how you did frighten me—and, oh my! thar's young Massa Bob!"

Juno had often come up to Bristol to see us, and felt an engrossing interest in all of the family. She now led me into the house, and went as briskly to work as her rheumatic old limbs would allow, to make a good fire—piling on logs, blowing with the bellows, and talking all the while with the volubility of a kind old soul of fully sixty years of age. My father had gone to tie up the horse under the shed until Clump should return and take care of him. Clump was Juno's husband, and her senior by many years. The exact age of negroes is always of unreliable tradition. The two had charge of the house, and were, indeed, rulers of the entire cape. Clump cultivated vegetables sufficient for his wife and himself, and was also a skilful fisherman. His duties were to look after the copses and fences and gates, and to tend the numerous sheep that found a living on the cape; in which tasks Juno helped him, besides keeping the old house free from ghosts and desolation—indeed, a model of neatness and coziness.

I must now pause for a minute and describe how it happened that the two old negroes were living on that out-of-the-way farm in Cornwall. My father had been a West Indian proprietor, and had resided out in the West Indies for many years. It was in the days when Wilberforce and true and noble philanthropists who fought the battle of emancipation with him first began to promulgate their doctrines. My father, like most other proprietors, was at first very indignant at hearing of proceedings which were considered to interfere with their rights and privileges, and he was their strenuous opponent. To enable himself still more effectually to oppose the emancipists, he sent for all the works which appeared on the subject of emancipation, that he might refute them, as he believed himself fully able to do. He read and read on, and got more and more puzzled how to contradict the statements which he saw put forth, till at length, his mind being an honest and clear one, he came completely round to the opinion of the emancipists. He now conscientiously asked himself how, with his new opinions, he could remain a slaveholder. The property was only partly his, and he acted as manager for the rest of the proprietors. They, not seeing matters in the light in which he had been brought to view them, would not consent to free the slaves and, as they believed, not unnaturally, ruin the property as he desired. Then he proposed having the negroes educated and prepared for that state of freedom which, he assured his partners, he was certain they would some day ere long obtain. They replied that slaves were unfit for education, that the attempt would only set them up to think something of themselves, and certainly spoil them, and therefore neither to this proposition would they agree. They were resolved that as the slaves were theirs by right of law—whatever God might have to say in the matter—slaves they should remain. At length my father determined, after praying earnestly for guidance, to have nothing personally to do with the unclean thing. Had he been able to improve the condition of the slaves, the case would have been different; but all the attempts he made were counteracted by his partners and by the surrounding proprietors, who looked upon him in the light of a dangerous lunatic. He therefore offered to give up his share in the property, provided he might be allowed to emancipate some of the slaves. To this even they would not consent, as they were afraid he might select the most able-bodied, and thus deprive the ground of some of its best cultivators. He did his best for the poor blacks, but the law was on the side of his partners, and, to do them justice, they, blinded by their interests and the contempt in which they held the negro race, considered they were right, and that he was wrong. All they would do was to allow him to select ten negroes from among a certain number whom they pointed out, and they agreed to pay him over a sum of money for his share of the land. To this proposal he was compelled to agree, and as West India property was at that time considered of great value, he received a very handsome sum, yet it must be owned not half what he might properly have claimed. With this he returned to England, and, as he was a man who could not bear to be idle, he commenced business as a general merchant at Bristol. Shortly after that he married, and my brothers and sisters and I in due course came into the world. Among the negroes he set free were Clump and his sable partner Juno, and so attached were they to him that they entreated that he would take them with him to England. Clump was, properly speaking, a free man; for having in his younger days, after he had married Juno, gone a short trip to sea, he was wrecked, and after meeting many adventures, finally pressed on board a man-of-war. He saw a good deal of service, (about which he was very fond of talking, by the by), and at last obtaining his discharge, or rather taking it, I suspect, with French leave—ever mindful of his beloved Juno, he returned voluntarily to a state of slavery, that he might enjoy life with her. The navy in those days was not what it now is, and he had not been in the enjoyment of any large amount of freedom. He had, indeed, being a good-natured, simple-hearted fellow, been sadly put upon both in the merchant service and navy. It was always, he used to say, "Clump, you don't want to go on shore, you stay and take care of the ship;" or, "Clump, you stay in the boat while we just take a run along the quay for five minutes;" or, "Clump, leave is no use to you, just let me have it instead of you;" or, "Clump, rum is a bad thing for niggers. I'll drink your grog to-day, and if you just tip me a wink I'll take half of it to-morrow, and let you have the rest, or Bill Noakes'll have the whole of it, and you'll get none." Clump and Juno being intelligent, trustworthy people, my father, as I have said, put them in charge of the farm on the cape, which they in a short time learned to manage with great judgment. Two other negroes he took into his service at Bristol. One of them became his butler, and it would have been difficult to find his equal in that capacity.

Now a lesson may be learned from this history. My father did what he considered right, and prospered; his partners, neglecting to enlighten themselves as they might have done, persisted in holding their black fellow-creatures in abject slavery, refusing one of the great rights of man—a sound education. Emancipation was carried, and they received a large compensation, and rejoiced, spending their money extravagantly; but the half-savage negroes whom they had neglected to educate refused to work. Their estates were left uncultivated for want of labourers, and they were ruined. My father, managing his mercantile affairs wisely, was a prosperous man.

His business on this visit was to see an adjoining property which had once belonged to the family, and which, being in the market, he hoped to repurchase.

The house had been built as long back as 1540-1550. It was of stone—the rough stone, as it had been taken from the beaches and cliffs, of different shades and kinds. Above the ground floor was only an attic storey; and the main part of the ground floor consisted of four large low rooms, panelled in wood, and with ceiling of dark, heavy beams. Adjoining the rear of these, my grandfather had built a comparatively modern kitchen; but every fireplace in the old house preserved the generous cheerful style of ample spread and fire-dogs. From the great door of the main floor a narrow stairway, like cabin steps, led up, with quaintly carved banisters, to five real old-fashioned bedrooms, rising above to the ridge of the steep-sloping roof and its uncovered but whitewashed rafters. The windows were at least five feet above the floor, and had the many small panes we sometimes yet see in very old houses. No doubt it was a house of pretension in its day. When I was a boy it remained a precious ark of family legends and associations. How splendid it is to possess a house nearly three hundred years old. To-day nothing could induce me to exchange the walls of that dear old house for the handsomest residence in Belgravia. A house can be built in a few months; but to make a home—that is beyond the craft and quickness of masons, carpenters, and architects.

Alone on that bold, sea-beaten cape, so sturdy, dark, and time-worn, it looked out always with shrewd, steady little window-eyes on the great troubled ocean, across which it had watched the Pilgrim Fathers sailing away towards the new home they sought in the Western world, and many a rich argosy in days of yore go forth, never to return. It might have seen, too, the proud Spanish Armada gliding up channel for the purpose of establishing Popery and the Inquisition in Protestant England, to meet from the hands of a merciful Providence utter discomfiture and destruction. With satisfaction and becoming dignity, too, it seemed on fresh sunny mornings to gaze at the hundreds of sails dotting the sea, and bound for all parts of the globe, recalling, perhaps with some mournfulness, the days of its youth and the many other varied scenes of interest which it had witnessed on those same tossing billows from its lofty height.

All through our supper, which was laid in the largest of the first floor rooms, did Juno stand by, repeating the refrain—

"Oh dat nigger, dat Clump,—why he no come? And here's Massa er waitten and er waitten; but Clump, ole mon, he get berry slow—berry, berry slow.

Now Massa Bob, vy you laff at ole Juno so?—hi! hi!"

However, Clump came at last; and when he beheld us, great and comical was his surprise. He dropped his basket to the floor, and, with battered hat in hand and both hands on his knees, stood for a moment and stared at us, and then his mouth stretched wide with joy and his sides shook with delight, while the tears trickled down from the wrinkled eyes to the laughing ivory.

"Tank de Lord! tank de Lord! Clump lib to see his ole Massa agin; and dat young gemmen,—vy, lem'me see! vy, sure as I'm dat nigger Clump, ef dat ain't—Massa Drake?—no,—Massa Walter?—no,—vy Juno, ole woman! dat are Massa Bob!" He took my hands and shook and squeezed them, saying over and over again, "Massa Bob am cum ter see de ole cradle. Oh! hi hi!"

Chapter Two.
The Dream confirmed by Reality.

Three years elapsed before I saw the cape again. Indeed the remembrance of that visit there, of a few days only, began to assume indistinctness as a dream, and sometimes as I thought of it, recalling the events of the journey there and back in the chaise, the wild scenery and the strange sound of the surf, the old dark house and the devoted black servants—sometimes, I say, as I thought of all these, as I loved to do when I settled myself in bed for the night, or when in summer I lay on my back in the grass looking up at the flying clouds, I would have to stop and fix my attention sharp, to be sure whether it ever had been a reality, or whether it might not be, after all, only a dream. I think my father was afraid of the fascination of the cape for us boys—afraid its charms, if we once partook of them freely, might distract our attention from the order and duties of school life. To be sure, we always went to the country with our parents for a month or six weeks, and enjoyed it exceedingly, laying up a stock of trout, squirrel, and badger stories to last us through the winter. But there was no other country, we imagined, like the cape; and as our father and mother never lived there, and rarely spent even a single night on the whole property, they thought it best, I suppose, that we should not run wild there and get a relish for what all boys seem to have, in some degree, by nature. I mean the spirit of adventure, and love of the sea.

However, the good time came at last, or a reliable promise of it first, just fifty years ago this very February. We older boys—Walter, sixteen years of age, Drake, fourteen, and I, Robert, twelve—were attending school at Bristol, and were, as usual too in the winter evenings, at work over our lessons at the library table, when, on one never-to-be-forgotten evening, our father, who was sitting in an easy chair by the fire, suddenly asked, "Boys, how would you like to pass next summer on the cape?" Ah! didn't we three give a terrific chorus of assent? "Jolly! magnificent! splendid!" we cried, while Walter just quietly vaulted over half a dozen chairs, two or three at a time, backwards and forwards, till he had expended some of the animal vivacity stored up in abundance within him. Drake, as usual when extremely pleased, tried to accomplish the rubbing of his stomach and the patting of his head both at the same time; and I climbed into the chair with my father, and patted his cheeks and thanked him with a fierce shake of the hands.

"Bob, boy, you are the only one of my youngsters who has been at the old place, and you must have painted it as a wonderful corner of the earth, that Walter and Drake should testify their pleasure in such eccentric ways.—And look here, Walter: when you wish to turn acrobat again, let it not be in this library or over those chairs; choose some piece of green grass out of doors.—Well, boys, perhaps you can pass the summer at the cape. I do not promise it, but shall try to arrange it so if your mother is willing; but under the unfailing condition that you make good progress in your studies until that time."

"Shall we all be there together, father, and for the whole summer, and without any school? How delightful!"

"Not too fast, Drake. Without school? What an idea! Why, in six months you would be as wild and ignorant as the sheep there. No; you shall have a strict tutor, who will keep you in harness, and help Walter to prepare for going up next year to Cambridge. But only you three will be there. I have some business in London, and I shall take your mother and Aggie and Charley with me."

During those February evenings there were many more conversations on the same subject, full of interest to us boys, and finally it was fully decided by our father and mother that we should go in May, and stay there until autumn; that a certain Mr Clare should be our tutor, and that Clump and Juno should be our housekeepers and victuallers.

Never did a springtime appear longer and more wearisome. We counted every day, and were disgusted with March for having thirty-one of them. What greatly increased our impatience and the splendour of our anticipation was that, some time in March, our father told us that a brig had been cast away in a curious manner on the shore of the cape, and that he had purchased the wreck as it lay, well preserved and firmly held in the rocks above ordinary high-tide. He proposed, at some future time, to make use of it as a sort of storehouse, or perhaps dwelling for labourers. A shipwreck! a real wreck! and on our cape! stranded on the very shore of our Robinson Crusoe-like paradise! Just imagine our excitement.

The particulars of the wreck were as follows:—A brig of 300 tons burden, on a voyage from South America to the Thames, having lost her reckoning in consequence of several days' heavy gale and thick weather, suddenly made the light on the Lizard, and as quickly lost it again in the fog which surrounded her. The captain, mistaking the light he had seen for some other well-known beacon, set his course accordingly. That was near nine o'clock in the evening. The wind and tide helped him on the course steered, and a little after midnight the misguided brig struck on a rock three-quarters of a mile south-west of our point of land. The wind had then increased to a gale, and was gathering new strength with every moment. In less than an hour the thumping and grating of the vessel's keel ceased, and then the captain knew that the rising tide had set him off the rock; but, alas! his good brig was leaking badly, and the fierce wind was driving her—whither the captain knew not; and in five minutes more, by the force of the wind and suction of the shore current, she was thrown high up on a rocky projection of our cape. One sailor was washed overboard by the breakers as she passed through them, and was dashed to death, probably in an instant, by the fierce waves. The next day, when the storm had abated, the body was found far above where the brig lay fastened immovably in the vice-like fissure of enormous rocks. Twenty sovereigns, which perhaps the poor fellow had saved to bring home to his old mother, were found in a belt around his waist.

The damaged cargo was removed, and the wreck sold at auction, my father being the purchaser.

There was an old church situated on the summit of a neighbouring point of land, and to its now seldom used churchyard the body of the poor sailor was conveyed. His grave was one of the first points of interest to us when our visit to the cape commenced; and many a time that season did I sit and watch the brown headstone topping the bleakest part of the sea-bluff, and as the great voice of the sea, dashing and foaming on the stony beach beneath, sang in its eternal melancholy grandeur, I fancied long, long histories of what might have been that sailor's life; and I wondered sadly if the poor mother knew where her son's grave was, and whether she would ever come to look at it. On the stone was written:—

Harry Breese

Lies Here, Near Where A Cruel Shipwreck Cast Him,

March 23rd, 1814:

Aged 24 years, 2 months, and 17 days.

Rest in peace, poor body;

Thy shipmate, Soul, has gone aloft,

where thy dear captain, Jesus, is.

By the 7th May everything was prepared for our departure. On the next morning early we were to start in the stage-coach, and, what had lately added to our brilliant anticipations, Harry and Alfred Higginson, two of our most intimate friends, were to go with us—to be with us all the summer, join our studies and our fun. But we were to separate from our father and mother, and from our dear sister Aggie and the little Charley—from all those dear ones from whom we had never been parted for a day and night before. We were to leave for half a year. All this, covered at first by the hopes and fancies we had built, and by the noise and activity of preparation, appeared then, when everything was packed, and we, the evening before the journey, drew our chairs about the tea-table. The prospect of such a magnificent time as we expected to have on the cape lost some of its brilliancy. Indeed, I positively regretted that we were to go. We boys were as hushed as frightened mice.

After tea, Drake and I got very close to our mother on the sofa, but Walter lounged nervously about, trying to appear, I think, as if such an affair—a parting for six months—were nothing to such a big fellow as he. Aggie came and held my hand. When our father had taken his usual seat, he and our mother commenced to give us careful instructions how we were to regulate our time and conduct during our separation from them; we were directed about our lessons, clothes, language, and play; to be kind and patient with Clump and Juno; and very particular were our orders about the new tutor, Mr Clare, to whom we had been formally introduced a few days before, and we were required to promise solemnly that we would obey him implicitly in every respect. Besides which our father delighted us very much by the information that he had engaged an old seaman, Mugford by name, once boatswain of an Indiaman, who had taken up his abode at the fishing town across the bay from our cape, to be with us often through the summer in our out-of-school hours; that he would be, as it were, our skipper—perhaps reside with us—and that he was to have full command in all our water amusements; he would teach us to swim, to row, and to sail. That last subject cheered us up a bit, and when I saw Walter, who was still walking up and down the room, going through a pantomimic swim, striking out his arms in big circles, right and left, I commenced to smile, and Drake to laugh outright. So our conference ended in good spirits. And then we all kneeled in family prayer, and that evening before the parting, as we kneeled and heard my father's earnest words, I realised fully, perhaps for the first time, how, more than parents or friends, God was our Father; how, though we were going away from home and its securities, yet God was to be with us, stronger and kinder than any on earth, to guard and care for us.

During the few days we had known Mr Clare, he had been with us constantly, but we had not decided whether to like him or not. He seemed pleasant, and was easy enough, both in his manners and conversation, but yet he had a calm and decided way that was rather provoking; as if to say, "I have read you through and through, boys, and can govern you as easily as possible." Now we had no idea of resisting him; we intended to behave well, and therefore his manner rather nettled us. However, there was not much to object to. His appearance was certainly all right—a large, bright, manly face and hearty smile, and a strong, agile figure. We five boys had talked him over, and at the last balloting our votes were a tie, for Walter declined to express an opinion yet whether Mr Clare was a "screw" or a "good fellow." Harry Higginson and Drake voted "screw," whilst Alfred and I said "good fellow."

We must pass over the "goodbyes" of the next morning. Let us imagine there were no wet eyes and sinking hearts. However it may have been, the big rumbling old stage-coach containing Mr Clare and five boys, and loaded well with trunks and boxes, rattled from our house in — Street at about six o'clock on that eighth morning in May, fifty years ago. Our hearts cheered up with the growth of the sun. By ten o'clock we were very talkative; by one, very hungry. The contents of a basket, well-stored by our mother, and put in just as we were starting, settled that complaint. The afternoon was tedious, and we were not sorry when the coach dropped us at the quiet little country inn where we were to sleep. I need not describe the journey of the next day. We were too eager to get to its termination to care much for the beautiful scenery through which we passed. As the evening drew on the weather became chilly. Ah! we were approaching the sea. By nine at night innumerable stars were twinkling over a dusky point of land which seemed to have waded out as far as possible into the indefinable expanse mirroring unsteadily a host of lights. A strong, damp, briny breath came up to us, and a vast murmur as if thousands of unseen, mysterious, deep-voiced spirits were chanting some wonderful religious service. "Whoa!" with a heavy lurch the yellow post-chaise, in which we had performed the second day's journey, came to a stand. We had arrived before the old stone ark that was to be our home for half a year.

Chapter Three.
Introduction to our Salt Tutor and the Wreck.

It was on Wednesday night that we became the guests of Clump and Juno, and commenced our cape life. The next morning at breakfast—and what a breakfast! eggs and bacon, lard cakes, clotted cream, honey preserves, and as much fresh milk as we wanted—Mr Clare told us that we need not commence our studies until the next week; that we could have the remainder of this week as holidays in which to make a thorough acquaintance with our new world.

Our first wishes were to see the wreck and old Mr Mugford, whom we agreed to dub Captain Mugford; and so, immediately after breakfast, we started out with Mr Clare to find those items of principal interest. When we had got beyond a hillock and an immense boulder of pudding-stone, which stood up to shut out the beach view from the west side of the house, we saw the wreck, only about half a mile off, and hurried down to it. Mr Clare joined in the race and beat us, although Walter pushed him pretty hard.

The brig sat high up on the rocky cliff, where only the fullest tides reached it. The deck careened at a small angle, and the stern projected several feet beyond the rocks hanging over the sea. The bow pointed toward the house. The brig's foremast only was standing, to the head of which old Mugford used to hoist, on all grand occasions, or on such as he chose to consider grand, a Union Jack or a red ensign, which had been saved from the wreck. The bowsprit was but little injured, and the cordage of that and of the foremast was there, and the shrouds—all of which had been replaced by old Mugford, who, having made the wreck his residence by my father's wishes, restored to it some of the grace and order the good brig possessed before misfortune overtook her, and now it looked fit for either a sailor or a landsman—a curious mongrel, half ship, half house. By the stump of the mainmast there stood a stove-pipe projecting from the deck.

When near the brig, which we always afterwards called by the name she had sailed under—Clear the Track—we hailed "Brig ahoy!" In a moment the head and shoulders of the Captain appeared above the companion-hatch, and his sonorous voice answered heartily, "Ah! ahoy, my hearties: this is the good brig Clear the Track; come aboard." He cast over the side a rope-ladder, such as is in common use on board ships, and we climbed to the quarterdeck, over the stern-board of which, and covering the companion-hatch, there had been built a roof, or open cabin, making that part of the brig answer the same purposes as the porch of a house. There were benches along the sides, a spyglass hanging overhead in beckets, and a binnacle close by where the wheel had once stood.

The Captain, as we will henceforth call him, however, just then fixed our attention more than the strangely fitted—up wreck. He was short, only about five feet four in height, with very heavy, broad, straight shoulders, immense chest, long arms, very narrow, compact hips, and short, sturdy legs, much bowed. His features were large, straight, and determined, and with something of the bulldog in them, yet stamped with kindness, intelligence, and humour—

a face that might be a terror to an enemy, as it was a surety to a friend. It was well bronzed by many a storm and tropical sun, and a dark beard grew on it, as the wild moss on the sea-rocks, in a luxuriant, disorderly manner. His hair was very thick, black, and glossy, only here and there flecked with the grey of age, and hung in curls that almost made his rough and powerful head even handsome. Walter said that night that he was sure Samson and Neptune were relatives, for without doubt the Captain was descended from both of them. With the jawbone of an ass he might put to flight a thousand Philistines, and with a trident drive a four-in-hand of porpoises.

We told that to the Captain afterwards, when we got to know him well, and it tickled him greatly. He declared it was the finest compliment he had ever received, and took Walter high in his favour from that moment.

Our new friend never wore either collar or vest. When not "on duty," as he expressed it, he went about in his shirt-sleeves. His breeches were of the ample sailor-cut, and hung from suspenders as intricate as a ship's rigging. His shirts were spotlessly white, and of very fine linen. A short black pipe was always in his mouth, or sticking its clay stem from a waist-band pocket.

Such, my dear boys, was Captain Mugford, whom we fellows dubbed "our salt tute," in contradistinction to Mr Clare, who was afterwards known as "our fresh tutor."

As Mr Clare came over the brig's side, he said, with a bow, "Captain Mugford, I believe. These boys are to be both your crew and my scholars. I am their tutor, Richard Clare."

"I am happy to see you, Mr Clare. Give me your hand, sir. I hope our different commands will not clash."

As the skipper shook hands, he looked Mr Clare all over at a glance, and smiled as if pleased with the inspection.

"Come here, boys; if I'm not out in my calculation, these boys will do to sail any craft on land or water! Well, my hearties, we are often to be shipmates, so let's be friends to start with. I don't know your different names, boys, only that three of you are sons of my old and respected friend and owner—that's good enough—and you all look as if you hated lies and kept above-board."

"These," said Mr Clare, laying his hands on Harry's and Alfred's shoulders, "are Higginsons!"

"Higginsons? Fancy I knew your father, young gentlemen—an honest man, and a kind man, and a true man, and a brave man, if he was John Higginson; and brother of David Higginson, under whom I once served, and a better sailor never stepped. As he died unmarried, I take you to be John Higginson's sons. And if all you boys act as honest as you look, you need not care for shipwrecks of any kind—love or money, lands or goods, by land or by water."

Well, we thought the Captain a brick. So he was. So he proved.

We passed all the morning on the wreck. Each one of its details was a new delight. The Captain talked about the brig as if she were a human being in misfortune. An old invalid, he said—a veteran old salt laid up in a sailor's snug harbour; laid up and pensioned for the remainder of life, where it was able to overlook, by the side and in the very spray of its well-loved brine, the billows it had often gloried in.

We went below to the Captain's cabin and stateroom. There everything bore the marks of a sea habitation, and when hearing the dash of the waves on the shore and listening to the Captain's talk, I could not help fancying myself on a voyage. Not a nook or hole of that vessel but we explored, and numberless questions had each one of us to ask. Mr Clare seemed as much pleased and interested as we were. When at play, indeed, he was as heartily a boy as any of us.

Great was our astonishment—Mr Clare, however, was prepared for it—upon going between decks, where the cargo had once been stored, to find ourselves in a schoolroom—a long, low schoolroom. Thick glass windows, only about eighteen inches square, had been set in on each side, and protected with dead-lights to fasten tight in case a heavy surf should dash up so high, and the entire hold—where on many and many long voyages there had been stored, in darkness, spices, coffee, sugar, and perhaps gold and jewels—was now transformed to a schoolroom.

There was a long table and there were globes and maps, shelves of books, and a blackboard. That schoolroom had, I am sure, none of the dulness and repulsiveness of other schoolrooms to us. No; it rather seemed a delightful place—an Arabian Nights' sort of study, with a romantic salty influence pervading it to comfort us at our tasks. We could take hold there of geography and history. Mathematics in a vessel's hold, what was it but a foreshadowing of navigation? We felt no hostility to Latin and Greek, for we were but reading of foreign lands and strange people across the ocean in old times, the occurrences of which were but storm-cast hulks like our old brig.

So low was our roof, the deck, that the crown of Walter's cap touched it, and Mr Clare had to bend his neck when he moved about. The square, dwarf windows looked out on nothing but jagged rocks and rolling blue waves.

Away forward and aft our schoolroom was dark, and the distance between decks so narrowed that we could only explore those extremes of the hold by going on hands and knees—with the chance, too, of starting some big rat, an old grey navigator, perhaps, who, believing firmly in "Don't give up the ship!" could not get over his surprise at seeing his once rolling and well-stored residence now stationary, and furnishing no better victuals than book-leaves, chalk, and sometimes the crumbs of a boy's lunch. I imagined the crew of old rats assembling beneath the globes at night, when a moon streamed through the small windows; and the captain, a surly grey fellow, with long whiskers and brown, broken grinders, taking his place on a Greek lexicon, and then the speeches of inquiry and indignation shrilly uttered in the mass meeting. "Long tails!"—would commence some orator with a fierce squeak—"long tails, long tails, I say! what in the name of all that's marine does this mean? Cheese and spices! how things are changed. Will this craft never sail, and our parents waiting for us in the New World over the sea! Where is our 'life on the ocean wave'? where is, I say, where 'a home in the rolling deep'? Can it be that our young are no longer to be nourished on sago, rice, or maize? Alas! if it has come to that, I myself will gnaw the beard from the old curmudgeon who thinks he sleeps here safely. Is the degradation of effeminate land rats, cheese-eaters, wharf robbers, stable vermin, to come upon us? Fates forbid it! Soon, perhaps, some fierce tabby may come to make our once brave hearts tremble. Then, then,"—but I imagined the eloquence broken off there and giving place to a furious scamper, as perhaps old Captain Mugford, arrayed in a long nightshirt and red bandanna nightcap, would fling open his stateroom door and send a boot-jack flying amid the noisy, noxious animals.

To think that our schoolhouse was on such a wild seashore—in a wrecked vessel, the same craft in which poor Harry Breese, who rested in the churchyard near by, had voyaged and been lost from—to have the smell of tar, and be surrounded by a thousand other sailor-like associations. What a glorious school-house, that old wreck by the ocean! What boy ever had a finer one!

The afternoon of that first day of novelty on the cape I remember with minute distinctness. We strolled about the beaches and climbed the rocks, everything being marvellous and delightful to us. In the evening Captain Mugford came in, and Mr Clare and he talked whilst we boys listened. After the Captain had gone, Mr Clare read the evening prayers to us, and that grand Psalm, the one hundred and seventh. The words reached us with the noise of the waves they sang of:—

They that go down to the sea in ships,

> that do business in great waters.

These see the works of the Lord,

> and His wonders in the deep.

For He commandeth, and raiseth the stormy wind,

> which lifteth up the waves thereof.

They mount up to the heaven, they go down again to the depths:

> their soul is melted because of trouble.

They reel to and fro, and stagger like a drunken man,

> and are at their wit's end.

Then they cry unto the Lord in their trouble,

> and He bringeth them out of their distresses.

He maketh the storm a calm,

> so that the waves thereof are still.

Chapter Four.
Captain Mugford's Saturday Lesson.

With a new week commenced our studies—order in tasks and play taking the place of the licence and excitement of the first days of novelty.

By Mr Clare's rule we reached our school-house in the wreck every morning at eight—that is, every morning except Saturday and Sunday. The brig's bell was our summons. Captain Mugford struck it as punctually as if the good order and safety of a large crew were dependent on his correctness. Our school-hours continued until half-after one. The remainder of each day was our own, only subject to the general directions of Mr Clare and the instructions of Captain Mugford in boating. Of course that was no task—rather the very best sport we had. Mr Clare grew fast in our good opinions. He was strict; but boys do not dislike strictness when it is mated with justice and guided by a firm and amiable disposition, as it was with our tutor.

We soon got to see that Mr Clare, in his way, was as much of a man as Captain

Mugford, and that the Captain respected him highly. The Captain always liked to have an evening smoke with our tutor, and the boating excursions were much jollier when Mr Clare made one of the party, as he often did. He was our master in school, but only wished to be our companion in play. In every athletic exercise he excelled, and I dare say that was one great reason of the powerful influence he soon gained with us—for boldness, strength, and agility are strong recommendations to boyish admiration. About two weeks after the commencement of our cape life, as we were going to bed one night, "our fresh tute" became the subject of discussion; and our first opinions were changed by a vote, in which all but Drake joined, that Mr Clare was a regular brick. Drake had a prejudice against tutors that required more than two weeks to break up. He allowed that Mr Clare seemed a very respectable sort of fellow, but then he said—

"I can't join in all the praise you boys give him; now my idea of a 'regular brick' is our 'salt tute.' He's the sort of man for me. If Captain Mugford only knew Latin and Greek!"

Mr Clare was from the north of England. His parents being poor, he had obtained his education under difficulties, and did not enter college until he was twenty-three years of age. His parents had emigrated when he was a child to Canada, where he had seen a good deal of wild life among the Indians. For some cause his father returned—to take possession of a small property, I believe—and brought him with him. After the common country schooling he could pick up in winter, he began to prepare himself for college in the hours he was off work on his father's farm, or had to take from sleep. So he had a life of some difficulty and adventure; and now, in his own hours, he was studying to become a clergyman. Notwithstanding such a boyhood of labour, his manners were good and agreeable, and no one would ever have guessed that his training until he went to college had been little above that of a farm servant.

It was some time before we made acquaintance with the sailing-boat which had been provided by our father, for the first weeks of our new life were stormy and cold. What whetted our desire for a sail was that Captain Mugford would not even show us the boat. We would tease him, and guess at every mast we saw in the bay; but the Captain only laughed, and put us off with such remarks as "Keep your powder dry, my young hearties!" "Avast heaving! the skipper is dumb."

However, one fine morning the Captain steered into our breakfast-room before all the fresh brown bread and clotted cream and eggs and bacon had been quite stowed away. "At it, ain't you, boys, with forecastle appetites? Pitch in, old fellows; make the butter fly!" He had wished Mr Clare a good morning, sat down on a corner of a side-table, wiped his forehead with a great red silk handkerchief, and got his elbows well akimbo, before he directed the remark to us. There he sat shaking with a pleasant little interior rumble of laughter at our earnestness in the meal, and expressing his appreciation every few moments with, "Well! that's jolly!" which remark each time portended another series of sub-waistcoat convulsions. He got through laughing as we finished breakfast, and then each of us went up for a shake of his hand.

"Your cargoes are in. When do you sail?"

"O Captain! can we sail to-day?" we all cried, for the joke and his unusually radiant face signified something better to come.

"I have a fancy that way, if Mr Clare says yes. That's my business here this fine Saturday. Yes, Mr Clare? Thank you! the youngsters are mad for a trip under canvas. You will go with us, sir, I hope? Thank you again!—Scamper, boys, for your caps! Ha! ha! ha!—With your permission, Mr Clare, I will fill my pipe.—Juno! Juno! Ah! there you are. Do, like a good old woman, get me a coal out of your wood-fire—just such a red, round piece of oak as Clump always chooses."

Presently Juno trudged smiling back, with a hot coal held in the tongs.

"Here, massa! here, Capting, is de berry heart of de fire!" and laying it carefully in the bowl of his pipe—"dat, sar, will keep yer terbacker gwine all day."

"Thank you, marm Juno! We shall try and bring you home some fish for dinner. A ninety-pound halibut, eh?"

The Captain having performed that operation so very necessary to his comfort, we all sallied forth for the long-anticipated sail.

The cape was about three-quarters of a mile wide where our house stood—it being on high ground, about halfway between the ocean and bay-side. The ground fell gradually in wavelike hillocks in both directions, and its chief growth was a short fine grass on which the sheep throve well. Here and there we saw them in little companies of eight or ten, but before we could get within fifty yards they scampered off in a fright, so unaccustomed were they to strangers.

Soon we descried a boat with pennant flying at moorings just off the bay shore before us. That, the Captain told us, was our "school-ship."

"And now come, boys," said he, "let us see which one of you will be the best hand on watch when we sail a frigate together—let us see which one can first read the boat's name; it is on the pennant."

At that distance we were all baffled.

"Well, try ten yards nearer; there, halt. Now try."

We all strained our eyes. I thought it read, Wave.

"No, Robert, it is not Wave.—Come, boys, sharpen your eyes on the sides of your noses, and try again."

"I can read it," shouted Harry Higginson, throwing up his hat. "Youth! Youth! —that's it."

"Yes, that's it. Hurrah for you, Master Harry! I promote you on the spot captain of the maintop."

We hurried down to a white sand-beach on which lay a punt. In that the Captain pulled us, three at a time, out to the Youth. When well under sail and standing out for more open water, our good skipper at the tiller, having filled his pipe, rolled up his sleeves, and tautened the sheet a bit, said—

"Boys, this craft is yours, but I am Commodore until each and all of you have learned to sail her as well as I can. May you prove quick to learn, and I quick to teach. But as I'm an old seadog, my pipe is out already. Give us a light, shipmate?"—I was trying with flint and steel to strike a few sparks into our old tinder-box—"there!—puff—puff—puff—that will do. I must talk less and smoke more."

As the jolly Captain got up a storm of smoke, slapped me a stinger on the knee, and winked at the pennant, Mr Clare jumped up, and swinging his hat, cried—

"Boys, let's give cheers, three rousing cheers, for our brave boat, the Youth, and her good master, Captain Mugford!"

And didn't we give them!!!

Chapter Five.
Bath Bay Lesson—The Midnight Council.

June came before we had made acquaintance with all the corners of our little new world. Every day it grew in interest to us, and, with the increasing fine weather, was the most beautiful spot on earth in our eyes. Once a week one of us was allowed to go over to the town with Clump, in his rowboat, and get letters from the post-office. That opportunity was always improved to purchase stores of groceries and other requisites. Each one's turn to be commissary only came once in five weeks.

Clump enjoyed those trips as much as we did. He would have meat or other things to get for the table, but would always reach the boat first in returning, and when he saw his "young master?"—as he called each of us boys—coming down the wharf loaded with a week's supply of various things, the old darky would commence to grin and slap his sharp knees, the slaps growing quicker and the grin breaking into "yha! yha! yhi!" as we drew near enough to show him our different purchases.

There was always a new pipe or a paper of tobacco for Clump, which he would lay on the seat beside him, and then put out the oars and pull with long, slow sweeps for our neck, each swing accompanied by a grunt, which, however, did not break the conversation he carried on, chiefly telling us stories of my father when he came as a boy, which often lasted till we reached our destination. Many a frolic and adventure would he thus relate with great gusto, and he had generally, too, some remembrance of my grandfather to repeat.

About the twentieth of June, the water was warm enough to allow us to bathe, and then began that exercise, the most useful and most wholesome, and perhaps among the most manly that a boy can practise.

Walter and both the Higginsons could swim. Drake and I were beginners. Captain Mugford was our teacher. He chose a little bay within, as it were, the large bay on the neck end of our cape. Bath Bay, as we named it, was about two hundred and fifty yards long, and sixty to seventy yards wide. Its shores were rocks, except at its bow end, where a soft beach sloped gradually for forty feet from the shore. About fifteen feet beyond our depth the Captain had anchored a stationary staging, which was merely an old flatboat caulked and floored over. It had steps and ropes from its sides, and was intended as the first object to reach and rest on when we had learned to swim a dozen or more strokes. Farther on, halfway the length of Bath Bay, was a large flat rock, which stood at high-tide two feet above water. Its sides were almost perpendicular, and were made accessible in the same way as "Youngster's Wharf." By that name those who could already swim called our staging near the beach. Leander's Rock, for we had a name for everything, had a depth of nearly thirty feet, and a finer place for diving cannot be imagined. Bath Bay was shut in by its wall-like sides and a bluff behind the sand-beach from all the severe winds, but after a storm out at sea we would get an even swell that was very pleasant to float on.

Our time for bathing was between the close of school at half-after one and our dinner-hour, three. All through the season, until early in October, we never lost a bath unless rain was falling heavily, so greatly did we enjoy it under the Captain's care. He would not have bathing-houses for us, as he said that the sun-bath after a swim was almost as good as the salt water itself. The Captain was always near the swimmers, in his punt, that in case of accident his assistance might be immediate.

Boys, if you have ever read Benjamin Franklin's directions to those learning to swim, you will understand the methods our Captain pursued to teach us. In his boat he was always dressed in bathing-clothes, and would often jump out to show us by example how to swim under water, how to float, how to dive, etcetera. I can assure you we enjoyed that sport as much as any we had, and before many weeks had passed we could all swim a few strokes. By the close of the season, I, the youngest pupil, could swim out to Leander's Rock, dive from it twenty feet deep, and swim ashore again easily. But more about Bath Bay, and our adventures there, hereafter.

After our baths and Juno's nice dinners we usually went to sail, and in a few weeks the Captain let some of us take the helm, he sitting by to instruct us, and to remedy, if need be, any mistake of the young sailor who happened to be our skipper at the time. Sometimes, instead of sailing, we would row in an excellent boat which we had for that purpose, and, four of us being at the oars, try how quick time we could make from point to point of the shore. With such practice, we made rapid improvements and by the middle of July could row a mile in twelve minutes; a month before we could only do that in twenty minutes. Sometimes Mr Clare and the captain took oars in our boat; at other times they rowed against us in the Captain's punt. That was glorious fun, and how we fellows did strive to beat our tutors, and often came very near it too—so near that we determined, if there was any merit in Try, to do it yet.

One night—it was about the 2nd of June, if my memory serves me—when we had gone up to our rooms for bed, and got undressed, Walter, who had been very quiet ever since our row in the afternoon when our tutors contended with and beat us as usual, called us to order, that we might organise, he said, as a regular boat club. We answered, "Good!" "Good!" and each boy, putting a pillow on his footboard, took a senatorial seat—each boy arrayed in the flowing cotton nightgown. When silence ensued, Walter addressed us in his energetic, determined way, but lowered his voice that not a whisper of our deliberations might reach the ears of Mr Clare, who was only separated from us by a partition.

"Fellows, we must beat our tutes—we must beat them, that is what I say. Let's get our boat in good order immediately—let's call her the Pupil—let's row every day, but not alongside of our adversary—no, no!—but where we can't be seen, and for two hard hours each day. And I move we have a coxswain, and that Bob be the boy—he is small, quick, and cool. Let's challenge our tutes to-morrow for a race."

"Agreed—agreed! hurrah!" we all shouted.

"For a race, I say, on, let me see, the anniversary of the glorious battle of Waterloo."

"Grand! splendid! hurrah!" were our interruptions again, and Drake expressed his delight by taking the pillow from beneath him, and slinging it with tremendous speed at Alf Higginson's head, who in consequence fell off his perch like a dead squirrel from a pine-tree. Alf fell heavily on his side, and we roared with laughter; but he was up in a moment, and rushed at Drake with a bolster. Walter, our dignified chairman, swooped down from his perch in a second, and catching the incensed Alfred by the extremity of his flying robe, slung him under a bed.

"Order! Order, boys!" he cried. "Pretty fellows you are to hold a meeting. You, Drake! pitch any more pillows, and we'll slide you out of the window. There, stop your racket! Mr Clare is up. Before he comes hurry up and say, all together, 'We will beat.'"

"We will beat," was responded as fiercely as if life was at stake, and, as Mr Clare opened the door to ascertain what was the disturbance, five innocent boys were under blankets and apparently sleeping the deepest slumber. Drake had even reached a regular bass snore. The moonlight streaming in the room, and which showed us a smile breaking irresistibly on Mr Clare's face, was not more placid than we. The door had hardly closed behind Mr Clare before Harry Higginson had sprung from his bed, and, almost on the space our tutor had stood a half second before, was enacting a ridiculous and vigorous pantomime of kicking our "fresh tute" from the room. As quickly the door opened again, and before Harry could get a single limb in order, Mr Clare had him by the arm. But the whole affair was too humorous for even Mr Clare's dignity. He could only say "So you are the noisy one, Henry Higginson. You can get in bed now as quickly as you got out of it, and to-morrow, when the afternoon's study is done, recite to me fifty lines of Virgil—from the twentieth to the seventieth line of the first book."

With that, Mr Clare went from the room, and Harry, with a low, long, whistled "phew," sought his bed disconsolately.

The next day after lessons I, as coxswain, by Walter's order, handed copies of the following note to Captain Mugford and Mr Clare:—

"Cape —, June 3, 1816.

"Messrs Mugford and Clare,

"The oarsmen of the galley Pupil would hereby challenge the gentlemen of the boat Tutor to a race on the eighteenth of June, in Bath Bay waters. The course to be from Youngster's Wharf around Leander's Rock, and return. Stakes to be —the championship of Bath Bay. The oarsmen of the Pupil would respectfully propose three p.m. as the hour for the race, and the firing of a gun the signal for the start. The oldest inhabitant, Clump, offers his services as umpire, referee, judge, and signalman.

"All which is submitted for the acceptance and concurrence of the gentlemen of the Tutor.

"(Signed) Walter Tregellin, Henry C. Higginson, Drake Quincy Tregellin, Alfred Higginson, Oarsmen,

"Robert Tregellin, Coxswain."

Mr Clare, when he read it, smiled and said he would see about it, and then turned to Henry and asked him if he had learned those fifty lines yet.

Captain Mugford was presented with his copy as he entered the house for dinner. "Hu–um!" he said, as he took the note in the hand with his hat, and wiped his red, wet forehead with an immense silk handkerchief printed with the maritime flags of all nations. "A note! Who writes me notes? Some of your nonsense, boys, eh?" So he hitched up his trousers and sat down on the doorstep, placing the red handkerchief in his hat beside him. "Let's see!"

"Good! good! that's very good. The middies have got their courage up. The idea of such a stiff old seadog racing with you youngsters!"

"But you will though, won't you, Captain, and make Mr Clare, too?" said Harry.

"Perhaps, boys, if Mr Clare will join, and then we will make you smart. And I tell you what, young gentlemen, if you beat I'll give you a splendid Malay race-boat that I have had stored in my ship-loft these three years."

"Hurrah! Captain, we shall win the boat!" we all cried.

"Ha! ha! what boys for warm weather! You talk as brave as a west wind. But I smell Juno's cooking; let's go in and talk it over with Mr Clare and a warm dish of stew."

It was all settled to our satisfaction before dinner was over. Mr Clare enjoyed the thing as much as the Captain, and declared they would have to practise together once a week. As for us, we never missed our two hours' pull every afternoon, rain or shine, blow high or blow low, until the all-important day proposed for the race.

Chapter Six.

Dissensions in Camp.

For every afternoon of those beautiful June and July days we rowed for two hours, from five to seven. Our studies were not relaxed in the morning, and our hours for swimming were regularly enjoyed, but the absorbing topic of thought and conversation was the approaching boat-race. Twice on Saturday afternoons we had seen Captain Mugford and Mr Clare pulling in their boat. They did not condescend to practise oftener, but we noticed that they worked in earnest when they did row. With the confidence of youth we feared not, feeling sanguine that we must beat them.

There was a vein of discord, however, in our little colony. Alfred Higginson and my brother Drake, who only differed by a few months in age, in other respects differed greatly, and had never been able, since our first acquaintance, to get along together. Alfred Higginson was of a nervous, sensitive disposition, quick in temper, and easily provoked. His tastes were fastidious. He was an excellent scholar, (much better than my brother Drake), and very fond of reading. He entered fully into all our sports, but preferred fishing, sailing, and swimming to our rougher harder amusements. He drew excellently, landscape and marine views and figures. He was a healthy, active boy, and could beat us all in running. I have said his was a quick temper, but it was a forgiving one. If he laughed not as loud and often as many of us, he caused us to laugh oftener than any, for he had a quick dry humour and witty tongue. When it came to chaffing, he was always conqueror.

My brother Drake was entirely unlike Alfred Higginson. He was a hardy, rough, jolly boy, overflowing with fun and animal life, what is called a "regular boy." Never quiet—laughing, singing, whistling all the time, heels over head in everything, pitching into his studies as irrepressibly as into his games, but with more success in the latter, though he was a fair student; better in his mathematics and other English studies than in the languages. The only reading he cared for was that of travel and adventure, voyages of whalemen and discoveries, histories of pirates, Indian scenes, hunting stories, war histories, Walter Scott's novels, "Gulliver's Travels," and the unequalled "Robinson Crusoe." Everything he could find about the Crusaders he revelled in, and even went at Latin with a rush when, Caesar and Nepos being put aside, the dramatic narrative of Virgil opened to him, and the adventures of the Trojan heroes became his daily lesson. But that he had to feed his interest, crumb by crumb, painfully gathered by dictionary and grammar, made him chafe. He enjoyed it, though, with all of us, when, after each day's recitation—after we boys had marred and blurred the elegance and spirit of Virgil's eloquence with all sorts of laboured, limping translations, that made Mr Clare fairly writhe in his chair—our tutor would drop a word of commendation for Walter's better rendering of the poem, and then read the lesson himself, and go over in advance the one for the next day. Then the ribs and decks of our schoolroom in the wrecked brig melted away as the scenes of the Aeneid surrounded us. The dash of the waves we heard was on the Trojan shore, or the coast of Latium, as we wandered with storm-tossed Aeneas. Or we walked the splendid court of Dido, or were contending in battle with the warlike Turnus for our settlement in Latium. Turnus and the fierce Mezentius were Drake's favourites. He never liked Aeneas, who was always Alfred Higginson's hero. Those readings were often disturbed by Drake's exclamations. His overflowing, outspoken disposition could not be restrained when his interest was powerfully enlisted; and as Mr Clare read, in his clear, impassioned manner, some exciting passage, Drake would shout out an exclamation of encouragement or satisfaction with a favourite warrior, and bring down his fist on the desk, as another favourite was discomfited or came to grief. I remember very well how often Drake was reproved for such unseasonable enthusiasm, which always caused an after sarcasm or witticism from Alfred Higginson; and I distinctly recall how, notwithstanding the formality of school-hours, when we came to the single combat between Aeneas and Turnus, and the death of the latter, Drake flung his book from the table, and shouted out in an angry voice, "I'll bet anything Virgil tells fibs!"

Those readings were treats to all of us. Drake having told Captain Mugford of them, and discussed the incidents that vexed him with the Captain, got him so interested that he asked Mr Clare to allow him to come in at the close of our recitations. Of course that favour was readily granted, and after that time the Captain always made one of the auditors. He used to laugh and shake over Drake's excitement, and yet entered into it himself, and I have seen salt drops running down his cheeks and Mr Clare's, as the latter rendered in a voice slightly trembling some of the pathetic passages in which Virgil is so exquisitely beautiful.

I am glad to write of those lessons in the old brig's carcass, for they are remembered so pleasantly. Moreover, it came naturally in drawing my dear brother Drake's character, and the effect of those heroical classics influenced, in a manner very quixotic, the crisis of the continued quarrel between Drake and Alfred Higginson, to which we are coming. The great dissimilarity in the characters of the two was a reason for their want of sympathy and agreement, one with the other, but the causes of the open warfare which existed between them were the faults of each—the irritability, slight conceit, and stinging tongue of Alfred Higginson; the teasing practices, want of toleration for the feelings and peculiarities of others, and a certain recklessness of Drake's. And yet they were both noble boys, with nothing false or ungenerous or underhanded about either of them.

Ever since we had come to the cape, their skirmishes of words and disagreement had been continual, and several more tangible collisions, where blows had been exchanged between them, were nipped in the bud by Walter and the others of us, and once by the Captain, who, wrought up by their quarrelsomeness, separated them pretty fiercely, and, holding each at arm's length, told them that, if there was any fighting to be done among his crew, he must have a hand in it. Then he laughed one of his bars of rollicking "ha-has," and dropped the boys with the injunction that if they had another "mill," he should certainly let their fathers know. "Now, boys, try if you cannot get along better, and when you have a quarrel again, bring it to Mr Clare or to me, and we will settle it better than your blows and frowns can do."

You remember how Drake knocked Alfred from the footboard of his bed on the occasion of our night meeting to get up the boat-race. That was a good example of Drake's reckless rudeness, proceeding merely from his boisterous disposition, but somehow those outbreaks were always directed to Alfred, just as the rough points of Alfred's disposition were sure to be turned to Drake. That fall had hurt Alfred, and from the date of the commencement of our boat-practice, the war between the two had waxed hotter and hotter. The contest seemed only to amuse Harry Higginson, but Walter—our mentor, my conscientious, tender-hearted brother, who led us all in games as well as in lessons—worried over it, and each day he exhorted the two to govern their tempers, and, with great tact and decision, whenever he saw a storm brewing, managed to throw oil upon the waters. However, his influence did not heal up the difference, and in about a fortnight, a few days before the intended race, there occurred during our afternoon boat-practice a little row between the two antagonists, which proved a final skirmish before the severe but ludicrous battle which crowned the civil war.

We were rowing in Bath Bay as usual, Walter pulling the stroke oar, and Harry Higginson the bow, whilst Drake and Alfred held the intermediate positions, Drake sitting behind Alfred—that is, nearer the bow. I had my place at the tiller.

Alfred Higginson had made a very ridiculous blunder in a French translation that morning. Such a thing was unusual for him, and was such a comical one that it set the others of the class in a roar of laughter. Drake was so extravagantly affected by Alf's blunder that Mr Clare had to stop his laughter, which was half genuine and half pretence, by ordering him out of the room. Even then we heard him ha-ha-ing outside. Poor Alfred was terribly mortified, and did not recover his composure even when the school-hours were over, and the first greeting he received, on emerging from the house, was from Drake, who immediately mimicked Alfred's mistake, and performed a variety of antics supposed to proceed from convulsions of mirth. On the way to the boat, Drake continued to tease Alfred. Walter reproved him continually, and even took hold of him once to compel him to stop; but he was in one of his most boisterous moods, and was so very funny that he kept every one but Alfred in shouts of laughter. But Alfred lashed him with the bitterest satire, and, as they say, sometimes "made him laugh on the other side of his mouth," until by the time we had reached the bay Drake had subsided into silence, and the tight closing of his lips, and quick walk, proved that Alfred's sharp wit was more fatal than Drake's broad fun. Both of the boys rowed sullenly, and we all felt that a storm was brewing. In the final round, when we made the course at our best and timed the performance, so as to notice what improvement we were making, Alfred caught a crab with his oar, in consequence of which the head of Drake's oar hit him sharply in the back. The mortification of a miss stroke is enough to anger a boatman, but coming as it did after the morning's blunder in class, and made, too, a pain of the flesh by Drake's blow, it was too much for Alfred's temper, and as Drake increased the irritation by calling him an "awkward lout," and then mimicking the blunder of translation with the accompaniment of a shout of laughter, Alfred turned quickly, and hit his opponent a stinging blow in the face.

In a moment the two boys grappled each other, and in a shorter period than it takes my pen to write it, the boat was upset, and we were all in the water. The combatants still clung to one another, and disappeared together. The adage, however, that "discretion is the better part of valour," enforced by such a deep, cold plunge, bore proof; for the irate youths came to the surface apart, and we all struck out for the rocks, distant about eighty yards. We climbed like half-drowned rats up the shore, where the fight was not resumed. Its very strange continuation was postponed until the Saturday after the boat-race, which must be reserved for another chapter. We, however, read then, in the faces of the discomfited antagonists, as plainly as you read here—

"To be continued."

Chapter Seven.
Before the Boat-Race—Clump's Story.

The day before the eighteenth was a Monday. In consideration of beginning a week's study to have it broken off again on Tuesday, and because of the many preparations there were to make for the great day, Mr Clare gave us the two holidays. We had our swim and boat-practice on Monday morning, and then set to work to make arrangements for the next day, every one taking a part with real zest. First the boat was carefully hauled up on the shore, and turned over on a way of joists we had prepared for her. The bottom was then carefully washed, and, after that, thoroughly rubbed with the sand-paper—about an hour's work, at which we all had a hand. Having got the sides and keel beautifully smooth in that way, Clump brought a kettle of pure grease, which was placed over a little fire of driftwood, and when the grease had become liquid, Walter, with a large fine paint-brush, anointed the entire boat's bottom in a most painstaking manner. We boys stood by, entering into the operation, which was supposed to prove wonderfully efficacious in increasing our boat's speed, with great interest, and Clump bent over the kettle, stirring the oil, and puffing at the short stern of his pipe eagerly.

Grouped with such absorbing concern about the body of the boat, Walter moving slowly from stem to stern, and stern to stem, laying on the magic oil, (unctuous of victory to our noses), with steady sweeps, and the bent figure of black old Clump beside the caldron, from which rose a curling smoke, we must have made a tableau of heathen offering sacrifice, or some other savage mystery.

The all-important job was at length completed, and we left our ark of many hopes to rest until the exciting hour of the morrow.

Clump was a sharer in our great expectations. His heart was set upon our success. He had to fill his pipe again before we left the boat, and pulled at it nervously and wrinkled his black skin into countless puckers as he walked beside us, thinking of the vast interests at stake and listening to our excited conversation. As we left him to go over to the town for a small cannon we had borrowed to fire the signals, he touched Walter on the sleeve, and said in the most slow and earnest manner, as he drew the pipe from his mouth and knocked its ashes on the ground—

"An I'se to be judge an' udder ting you'se talk of, Massa Walter, eh? An I'se to fire de gun, eh? W–a–all, I'se an ole nigger, an my heart ees shree-veled up like, I s'pose, but my gorry, young massas, ef you don't beat, old Clump will jist loaden up do musket again an'—an'—an' but'is 'ed agin de rock! Yah, fur sure!"

Having delivered himself of that tragical decision in a manner mixed of sadness and frenzy, he hobbled off, amidst our laughter and assurances that we should never allow him to injure the rock in that way, to consult with Juno, and probably load his pipe again.

No noble lord, with his thousands of pounds wagered on the Derby or Saint Leger, or perhaps, rather, I should say on some of the crack yachts of the day, was ever half so excited as was this good old darky about our boat-race.

Under the escort of Walter, Harry, Alfred, and Drake, the cannon arrived in the afternoon, and, by their united efforts and the assistance of the Captain, was mounted before sundown on a heavy piece of timber in the Clear the Track's bow.

By night the flags, ammunition, and many other necessaries for the morrow's undertaking were in order and readiness for service.

After the day's work, and filled with anticipations of the eventful morrow, we felt no desire for our usual outdoor games that evening, but found seats on the great boulder beside our house, where Mr Clare was resting, and the Captain was enjoying his smoke. Old Clump, too, having finished his tea and swept out Juno's kitchen, loitered toward us with his comforter—the pipe—and edged up respectfully within hearing of our conversation. So we boys leaned on our elbows, looking out at the dimly defined water, sometimes lighted in streaks by gleams of phosphorescence where shoals of fish were jumping; or, stretched on our backs, we watched the shooting-stars hurrying with speed quick as thought from one part of the immeasurable blue to another; while our tutors talked earnestly of former times, and we heard the shrill calls of gulls and other sea birds, the occasional tender bleating of the lambs in the distant sheepfold, and the soft regular splash of a summer sea on the rocks, until the delicate young crescent had dozed slowly down to its bed in the ocean,—and we, profiting by example, sought slumber in the old dreamful attic.

Harry Higginson was the first one up in the morning. He shook us to our senses, and whispered to get out of the house quietly, that we might call our tutors with the cannon's voice. That was an acceptable proposition, and we were soon stealing down the creaking stairs, shoes in hand. Having put those on, seated by the door-stone, we started on a run for the Clear the Track. It was just light, the soft dawn of a warm summer's day—not yet half-past four. Walter said he would bet old Sol had already fired a gun in honour of the glorious battle won that day by England and her Allies, but so far off we could not hear it.

We got on board the wreck as carefully as we had quitted the house, and I, being delegated to descend to the Captain's cabin and steal one of the flannel powder cartridges, was soon creeping by the snoring Captain with my booty secured. It took but a moment to ram home the charge and pack it over with pockets full of wadding; and then Harry, our gunner, touched it off. As the old brig shook with the report, Alfred jumped to the bell, and the way that clanged was splendid.

"Boys," said Drake, who was shaking with the fun, "can't you see old topgallant sail down below springing up in his berth with a lurch and cracking his head against the beams, and our dignified fresh tute jerking those long, thin legs out of bed, and wondering what's about to happen this fine morning, and old Clump and Juno groaning out 'O de Lord!' and knocking their black pates together as they both try to get out of bed at the same instant. How jolly!"

An immense red bandanna handkerchief at that moment popped above the companionway—then a hearty, weather-marked face we well knew—then a portion of an ample East Indian nightshirt, which threw up a pair of arms and fired off a couple of boarding-pistols. The discharge was followed by a stentorian "Three cheers for the great and glorious battle won this day!—hip! hip! hurrah! hurrah! hurrah!" in which we fellows joined with a yell.

"Ah! you young rascals have got before me this morning, but this afternoon it will be my turn—mine and Mr Clare's, you roystering middies!" and the Captain popped down again to finish his toilet.

We were soon joined by the Captain, and a little while after by Mr Clare, who was in the best of spirits, complimented us on our display of zeal and patriotism, and touched off the old gun once himself—"for practice," he said.

"But," continued the jolly old Captain, having taken Mr Clare's arm, "suppose we visit Ethiopia and see if a hot breakfast is not waiting for us there. These boys would rather stay here and load this cannon."

"No sir, no sir!" replied Harry, "we must load our own personal guns, for we mean to make our report this afternoon."

Laughing over that threat to our tutors, we went with them to breakfast, which we found ready as soon as our morning prayers were read. Clump brought in the dishes—Clump in uniform—and I never saw a funnier figure in my life. The coat was once my grandfather's—a colonel of West India Militia, I believe. Now my grandfather had been a rather short man, but very broad and stout, particularly round the stomach. Old Clump was tall and thin as a spectre, so the epaulettes fell over his shoulders, the waist flapped loosely eight inches above his trousers, and the short swallow-tails did not sufficiently cover the spot which the venerable darky usually placed on the chair to hide a patch, the bigness of a frying-pan and of a different material from the breeches themselves, that Juno's affectionate care had strengthened her liege lord's garments with—which garments, far more pastoral than military, and forced by suspenders as near the coat as Clump's anatomy otherwise would allow, failed by three inches of woollen stocking to meet his shoes. When you think how comical the excellent, old, white-woolled darky appeared, remember, too, that he was perfectly unconscious, until our laughter startled him, that he was not becomingly attired.

As our irrepressible appreciation of the fun was shouted out, Clump did not realise at first that he was its cause, but when he did all the pride and alacrity died from his face in an instant. In a bewildered, palsied way he put down the dish he carried, and, heaving a sad sigh, drew himself up until the rheumatic spine must have twinged, and, fixing his eyes on some point far above our head, stood in motionless dignity.

Even Mr Clare had laughed, but, recovering equanimity immediately that he saw how deeply Clump was wounded, he said:

"Boys, stop that laughing." He might have addressed his reproof to the Captain, too, for he was in paroxysms, and had his face buried in the countless flags of that great red silk bandanna of his. "Is it so very funny to see Clump doing honour to a day once so big with the fate of England and the world? Had the Allies been beaten at Waterloo, what might not have become of our beloved country? Instead of Napoleon being an exile in Saint Helena, he might have carried out his darling project of invading and humbling England to the dust. Though he cares no more for the Pope of Rome than does the Sultan of Turkey or the Shah of Persia, he would probably have established Popery with all its horrors and impositions, for the sake of more completely bringing our country into subjection to his will; and, once established, it would have been a hard matter to throw off its iron shackles. Boys, you do not sufficiently value your privileges as Englishmen and Protestants—or rather, I should say, as inhabitants of this free and favoured island of Great Britain. We are free to read our Bibles; we are free to worship God as we think fit; we are free to go and come as we list; we have a good constitution and good laws; we may think freely, speak freely, and act freely."

"Yes, Massa Clare; you may tell de young gemmen dey may laff freely too," broke in Clump. "I laff freely, I know, when I first set foot on de English land. I no longer slave, I free man, and so dey may laff as much as dey likes at ole Clump, perwided dey laffs wid him. I know one ting, dey would not have laff if dey had been in deir grandfather's coat when dis hole was made right through it into his arm." Clump held up his right arm and showed the bullet-hole in the coat, and what he declared to be the stain of blood still on it; and he then continued in a triumphant strain—

"Dis ole man Clump was 'is body-sarvant: but Clump was not ole den, and he follow his massa to de war—dat was long, long before dose young gemmen was born—afore dey was tinked of—and Massa Tregellin deir fader was young gemmen like dose, but more politer. We was sent wid de seamen to take de island of Martinique; and so we landed and looked bery fierce, and de Frenchmen thought we had come to eat dem; so dey say, no use fighting; and so, after firing a great many shot at us; but doing no harm, dey say when we land, 'We give in, we no fight more.' So we take de island, and no one hurt except one man scratch anoder's nose wid his bagonet, and make blood come. When de generals and de admirals see we done so well, dey say we go and take anoder island; so we all sets sail for to take Guadeloupe. Some of de ships got in one day, some anoder, and anchored in Grozier Bay. Ah, de enemy thought we come to eat him up, but dis time he stop. Dere was de frigate Winchelsea, of which Lord Garlies was de cap'en. He tun in, and bring his guns to bear on de shore, and under deir cover de soldiers and de bluejackets landed. Dere was a high hill, wid de fort full of French soldiers on de top of it. 'Dere, my brave fellow, we have to go up dere,' said de Kunnel. De seamen was commanded by Cap'en Robert Faulkner. He bery brave man. I could just tall you how many brave tings he did; how he lash de bowsprit of de enemy to his own mainmast, and neber let her go till he took her, and den was shot through de heart in de hour of victory. Well, de gen'ral say to us—'Now, boys, we don't want firing, but just let de enemy feel de cold steel. Dey don't like dat. Soldiers, use bagonets. Bluejackets, use your pikes and cutlashes.' 'Ay, ay, sir,' we shout; and den up de hill we go—up! up! De faster we go de better for us, for de French bullets come down peppering pretty sharp. We just near de top, and de enemy begin to look bery blue, when I see de Kunnel's right arm drop—he was only a cap'en den—his sword fell from his hand, but he seize it wid de oder hand, and wave it above his head, shouting, 'On, boys, on.' We reach de fort: de Frenchmen fire wid de guns, and poke at us wid de pikes, and swear at us wid deir mouds, and grapeshot and musket-balls come rattling down about our heads; but dat no stop us; and on we went till we got into de fort, and trou de gates, and den de Frenchmen, who had fought bery well, but could fight no more, rushed away. Just den I see de Kunnel look bery pale, just like one nigger when he frightened, and he goed round and round, and would hab fallen, but Clump caught him in de arms, and den Clump put him on de ground, and shouted for de doctor, and ran and got some water, and de doctors came and splashed water in de Kunnel's face, and he oped his eyes, and he say, 'Tank you, Clump.' Yes, de Kunnel, dis ole nigger's massa, tank him on de field of battle. When de dear Massa got better, he one day take de coat and say to me, 'Here, Clump, you and I went up dat hill, and it's a mercy we eber came down again. It's my belief if you hadn't got de water dat day to throw in my face, I should never have come round again; and so, Clump, here, take dis coat, I'll gub tur you to r'member dis fite.' And now dese gemmen laff at deir gran'pa's coat! but black Clump, ole nigger, lub it! Yaas, he'll lub it till he's 'posited in de bowels ob de arth."

The remembrance of my grandfather and that proud day for Clump, the keenness with which he had felt our rudeness, and the excitement of recital were, all together, too much for our good old castellan. The erectness of his figure gave way as he concluded, the enthusiasm in his features faded into dejection, and, as he turned from the table to leave the room, I saw a big drop, that had trickled down his wrinkled face, fall on his extended hand.

The cruelty of boys is an idiosyncrasy in their otherwise generous character. Of course there are mean boys, hard-hearted boys, cowardly boys; but Boyhood is more generous, open, tender-hearted, daring, than Manhood, yet its cruelty stands out a distinguishing trait. An old French teacher, loving children, wanting in dignity, broken in English, irritable in disposition; a sensitive young stranger, fresh from home, charming in innocence, sad with thoughts of a dear mother; a poor, frightened kitten, are all objects for boys' cruelty to gloat over.

And so, too, on the oddities of that dear old Clump, that excellent, noble-hearted old black man, who loved us with surpassing pride and tenderness, we delighted to prey on as vultures on a carcass, and yet, I am sure, we were neither vicious nor hard-hearted, but simply and entirely—Boys.

All this time, since our Saturday afternoon, when the fight overset our boat, Alfred Higginson and Drake had not spoken to one another. This eighteenth of

June, even, Drake did not wake Alfred, but left others of us to do so. Thrown together so intimately every minute of the day, and so often on the point of speaking—often almost necessitated to do so by circumstances, and frequently through forgetfulness—their unfortunate difficulty and enmity stole the freshness from their sports, and acted as a check and damper on the spirits of all our little company. However, the finale was not far-distant, but it was postponed until after the boat-race.

Chapter Eight.
The Regatta—The Duel.

By agreement we rested through the middle of the day, and, in place of our usual hearty dinner, took an early lunch. It was irksome, though, to be quiet when so excited, and when, too, a multitude of pastimes were suggested to our senses by the loveliness of that June day.

Mr Clare and Captain Mugford had gone to fish in the Race off the extreme point.

When half-past one o'clock came, Harry, who seemed the most impatient, proposed that we should go down to Bath Bay then, and wait there until three, the hour of the race. That we agreed to, but left directions with Clump to hurry our tutors up as soon as they returned, and have them ready for the race.

We had time to launch our boat carefully, and take a nice swim, before we descried our tutors, followed by Clump with a long musket, descending the knoll toward us. So we hastened our dressing, and, when they reached the beach, were ready to receive them in our extemporised costume of blue shirts and white trousers. Captain Mugford was already in a perspiration from his walk, and, what we boys also noticed with delight, seemed somewhat blown. However, he was jolly, and, flourishing the ever active handkerchief, proposed to Mr Clare that they should row round Leander's Rock, and let the boys follow them! "But at a respectful distance, remember, boys!" We laughed scornfully at his chaff. Harry touched his cap like a middy, and promised for our boat that it should keep at a very "respectful distance."

It took but a short time to complete preparations. Our tutors threw off hats, coats, and vests, and tied handkerchiefs about their heads. Then they lifted their boat into the water, and stood smiling at the excitement we could not help betraying. Clump was on his way to Youngster's Wharf, where, at the proper moment, he was to give the signal for starting by firing the musket. A flag waved from Leander's Rock; another was flying over our heads. The clear water of the bay soused in impatient little ripples against the boats we stood ready to enter, as if to say, "Well, why don't you come on?" and then, purling a few feet farther, skipped over the spar which was to be our goal. Clump had reached Youngster's Wharf. Seeing that, we entered our boats, seated ourselves carefully, balancing the oars ready to spring, and waited the signal. I alone could see Clump; the oarsmen had their backs to him. The long gun was brought up to his shoulder, and his eyes fixed on us. I saw his finger twitch, and as the hammer fell, my body gave way to help the start. The oarsmen, with their eyes on mine, acted in sympathy, and every oar touched the water; but the old flintlock had only snapped. How our adversaries laughed! The old man sprang about on the rock like a wounded baboon. He was indignant at the failure. Again we were in order. Again I saw the musket brought up. Bang! We were off, and were opposite Youngster's Wharf before the smoke had cleared from above Clump's head. The boats were side by side then. Notwithstanding the eagerness with which I swayed forward with every pull of the oars, and the frenzy that filled me, as in a moment more I saw our tutors' boat drawing slightly ahead, I had to laugh at the antics of Clump, who was rushing from side to side of his floating staging, dancing up and down like a rheumatic lunatic, tossing his arms wildly about his uncovered head, his face a kaleidoscope of grimaces, while he shouted to each one of us by name, in encouragement, in entreaty, in fear: "Oh, Massa Drake! pull, pull!" "Massa Walter! Massa Walter! dus you let 'em beat!" "Day'se gwine ahead! Oh dear! oh dear! oh dear!"

His voice was lost in another moment. We were nearly half across the bay, and our tutors' boat a full length ahead. I saw that my crew were too excited to do their best, so I called to them: "Boys, steady now! Keep cool, cool. Only think of what your arms are doing."

"There, that's better already! We're gaining! Hurrah! Stick to it!"

"Come, boys," called Mr Clare. "Come, we can't wait for you longer!"

I believe that lent five pounds of extra strength to every arm in my boat.

We were nearing Leander's Rock. Ay! and we were steadily gaining on our tutors.

They, too, saw that, but could do no better. Having a steersman, gave our boat an advantage of rounding the Rock closely.

We gained distance. In five minutes we were thirty or forty feet ahead.

But then, terrible to see, our adversaries made a spurt, and were coming up again, hand over hand.

They gained, gained, gained, until their stern was opposite Harry's oar-blade. I was almost wild with excitement. I called upon the boys, with every entreaty I could think of, to pull harder; urging on Alfred, who was evidently the weakest oar, and whose strength seemed waning.

But our tutors could not pull harder. They had done their best. Could we but keep our speed.

So we went, without widening or lessening the distance between us, for a hundred yards. But was it possible for us to hold out? How I prayed we might! We neared Clump again. The comic sight cheered me. Truly, if hopping about and entreaties could help us, what aid must that old nigger give us. I almost expected to see him soar off to us, he looked so like a crow taking flight.

"Fellows! keep a morsel of extra strength to use when we pass Clump, then just let us put forth our utmost breath and strength for those forty yards. But don't let our tutes gain. Look! look!"

But they were coming up—only by inches, to be sure, but coming.

We rushed past Youngster's Wharf. Clump stretched out his body as if to pull us on.

Hurrah! hurrah! Their bow is a foot beyond our stern.

"Hi! hi! hi! Yah! yah! Hurrah! hurrah! My young—"

Splash!!!

Clump had pitched in sure enough, head first. But there was no stop to our engines. Our tutors were four feet behind; but they were working with a last hope and mad effort.

"One more, boys!"

Cr–u–a–nk! we touched the spar, slid over its roundness as it sunk beneath our keel, and were on the soft beach—Victors!

We were crazy with joy, and completely used up. The boys jumped from the boat and threw themselves, laughing hysterically, on the sand.

Our tutors only said, in tones of mingled chagrin and exhaustion, "Boys, we are beaten, well and fairly;" and they pushed off again to pick up Clump.

I do not know any successes or honours of after-life sweeter or more satisfying than that boat victory.

Until bedtime, we remained just tired and happy enough to sit quietly and talk over the events of the afternoon.

In resuming study for the few days before Saturday, we had in anticipation for that time a fishing party on the rocks, for bass, which were beginning to bite sharply, and for which our bait was lobster and the crabs that were found under the small rocks at low tide.

In talking over the project together, Drake said he would not go this time, but would wait to see our luck. Alfred Higginson expressed neither assent nor dissent with the general arrangement, and of course we supposed he was to be of our party, until Saturday came and we were ready to start, poles, bait and basket in hand, when he was not to be found. We wondered at his disappearance, but had no time to hunt him up. Drake was there to see us off. The Captain and Mr Clare, who were going with us, told Drake they thought that boat-race had proved too much for him. He laughed, but was not as ready at an answer as usual. Indeed, he appeared rather low-spirited. However, we started on our excursion without a suspicion of the affair which prevented both fellows from joining it. It afterwards appeared that Drake had addressed the following note to Alfred Higginson on the day before the boat-race:—

"Cape —, June 17, 1816.

"Alfred Higginson,

"Our quarrels have gone nearly far enough, disturbing the peace of our entire company, and increasing the irritation between us. Let us conclude the dissension in a thorough and honourable way that may satisfy both and prove a final contest. After that I will agree to strive not to give offence to you, and also to bear silently whatever conceit and insults may escape you. Perhaps we may become friends. But we cannot remain as we are. The blow you struck the other day must be answered for. I ask satisfaction, and the incompleteness and vulgarity of a pugilistic encounter will not suit me. I propose, therefore, as we cannot resort to the regular duel of pistols, (for reasons so good and evident that I need not name them), that after the example of the ancients, whose history we are now daily reading, we have our combat. Arms of their fashion our ingenuity can supply, not of the same materials, I know, but of wood, which should prove effective enough for our purposes. I propose Saturday as the time, when those who might otherwise disturb our meeting are absent: and I propose the hold of the wreck as a suitable spot. Your sense of honour will, of course, keep this affair secret, and I ask a speedy reply.

"Drake Tregellin."

Only a warm, fierce, reckless-natured boy of fourteen could have hit upon such an absurdly quixotic way of deciding a quarrel. Indian combats between Red Indians in the Far West, the deeds of Sir Kenneth, Saladin, and Coeur de Lion in his favourite "Talisman," and the entire character of Drake's reading, had joined with and gathered romance from his late study of Virgil to misdirect an innate chivalry.

Alfred Higginson's reply was also characteristic:—

"Drake Tregellin,

"I have received your cartel. In my humble opinion nothing could be more stupid and silly than the resort you propose. I suppose you think your proposition very grand and chivalric. It endangers the continuance of our stay on the cape; it rebels against the rule we are under here; and it would make our parents unhappy. Its spirit of selfishness and indifference to everything but your own impulse is the same which causes and continues our quarrelling. But I shall be a fool with you this time. I have not the courage to balk your desire. I agree to the contest, if you agree to keep the peace after that. I suppose javelins and shields of wood are to be our weapons. What nonsense! But I shall be at hand, Saturday, at the brig, when the others have gone fishing.

"Alfred Higginson."

About an hour after we had got settled on Bass Rocks, and just as we commenced catching fish, and I had a mighty fellow slashing my line about and trying to snap the pole, we heard the voice of some one calling to us in distress, and, turning, saw Juno hurrying towards us as fast as her old limbs and breathless state would allow. She was chattering all the while, but it was impossible for us to understand the cause of her mission until she had come up to us and had taken a moment's rest. Then, the tears springing from her eyes and terror in her voice, she exclaimed: "De yun' gem'men—Massa Drake, Massa Alf'fed, dey is fiteten and tarr'en one udder to pieces. Dey is down dare in de ole ship and fire'en sticks and poke-en guns; an' oh Lord, I fear dey is all dead now!" Her excitement could no longer be contained, but broke forth in cries and ejaculations: "Oh! oh! oh! marssaful Hebbens! Oh de Lord, please top de yun' gem'men! Massa Clare, Massa Capting, ar'n't yous gwine? Ar'n't yous gwine afore dey is done dead? Dat dis ole woman mus' see such tings!"

We also gleaned from her, that, hearing a noise at the wreck, as she was passing near by, she had scrambled on board the vessel and there seen the two boys engaged in a severe fight; that she had hurried off for Clump, but could not find him; and that then she had run to where she knew we were; but we had to hasten her broken narrative to get at the whole matter, and then we all started for the wreck as fast as we could run, fearful that a tragedy was to meet our sight—that we might be too late to prevent it.

What a sight met our eyes as we hurried down the stairs to the brig's schoolroom!

Chairs, desks, and tables had been pushed back against the sides to make room for the duel, and there, in the so-formed arena, the atmosphere of which was thick with disturbed dust, lay in common confusion a split shield, two swords, a padded glove, a splintered lance, and a torn cap. The weapons—the shield in particular—reflected skill upon Clump or whatever carpenter had fashioned them. In some charge of one of the combatants, the round table, although intended to be in a place of safety, had been overturned, adding a globe, a streaming inkstand, and sundry books to the medley on the floor.

But our astonishment culminated when we saw Drake leaning back in Mr

Clare's big chair in the farther end of the hold, his head bleeding, a sleeve torn off, and an expression of comically blended fatigue and dignified indifference in his face, while near the opposite side of the schoolroom, and on one side of the stairway we had descended, was Alfred Higginson lying on the floor, his head supported on an arm, his countenance the picture of pain and mortification.

Evidently the battle was over. The parties spoke not a word; and the first exclamation that came from us was Harry's: "Hillo! A real duel, and no one killed."

Our good Captain, his face full of tenderness and anxiety, hurried to Alf and lifted him up, but as he was so much hurt as to be only able to hobble a few steps, Captain Mugford lifted him in his arms and carried him on deck.

"What is all this, my poor fellow?" asked the Captain, as he got him on a bench there.

"Rather a long story, Captain, but no one to blame but Drake and me. He ain't much hurt, is he?"

"That is what I want to ask you, Alf. Where is your pain?"

"There, sir, in my side. It is only stiff and bruised, but don't touch it hard, please. There! where your hand is. And I believe my hand is somewhat cut."

As it proved on examination by the doctor from the village, whom I brought over an hour afterwards, one of Alf's ribs was broken and the palm of his left hand badly gashed.

Whilst the Captain and Harry Higginson had attended to Alfred, Mr Clare and Walter took care of Drake. He was very laconic in his replies to their questions, and made light of the injury; but he was faint from the wound in the head, and his sleeveless arm was so stiff as to be useless to him then.

Juno, who had found Clump, joined us before we reached the house with our wounded comrades; but at the sight of Drake's bleeding head and Alfred carried in the Captain's arms, Juno's ejaculations recommenced, and Clump followed, only wringing his hands in mute despair.

Of the particulars of the fight we never knew further than I have related. Both of the principals in the affair hated to have it alluded to, and we spared their feelings.

When we had got them comfortably settled in their rooms, Mr Clare called the remainder of us aside and enjoined upon us that we should not question Drake and Alfred, nor mention the matter in their presence; and that in the meantime he would decide with Captain Mugford what steps to take when the boys had recovered.

In another week Drake was as well as ever, but hardly as noisy and reckless as of old. Alfred remained an invalid for some time longer.

When both were perfectly recovered, Mr Clare called us all together in the brig's schoolroom one afternoon, and then addressed us, particularly the two combatants, in a manner that I can never forget—it was so sensible, so manly, so solemn. He pointed out the faults of each, which had fed the long quarrel and finally serious conclusion. He painted the wickedness of that duel, (for it could be called nothing else), and all such affairs, which in former times were ignorantly considered necessary and honourable. He told us in what he thought true manliness, courage, and chivalry consisted. Then, in a simple, touching way, he suggested higher thoughts—our duty to our Father in heaven as brothers of one common family, and more than all of the example which our blessed Lord and Master set us while He was on earth—to forgive injuries—to overlook insults; and he spoke of charity as forbearance, and conquest as governing ourselves; and then begged us to join him in earnest entreaty to the Holy Spirit for the strength to practise that charity and make those conquests, to the Source whence such virtues came, and to the Ear which was never deaf to supplication. How simple and noble was that whole address! And I cannot forbear testimony to the fruitfulness of a Christian practice such as that of our then tutor, dear Mr Clare. Even thoughtless boys could not sneer at the constant manly practice of his life. We had to see that it gave the loftiest aims even to the smallest acts of his everyday life—that where he spoke one word he acted fifty in that service which ennobles the commonest deed. So that religion, which youth often regards as something whining and hypocritical, something only for the old and sick, we boys began to look up to as something which, if we could only partly understand, was, at the least, truly beautiful and noble.

The lesson and bearing of Mr Clare on that occasion was enforced by the fact that as he concluded, Captain Mugford, rubbing the back of a rough hand on his cheek for some reason, got up and crossed the room to Mr Clare, whose hand he took in both his, and said—

"Mr Clare, I am but a rough, wicked old sailor, but the words you have spoken to these boys have touched an older boy than they, and I thank you—I thank you!"

The parents of both Drake and Alfred were duly informed, by both Mr Clare and the boys themselves, of the affair.

From that time Drake and Alfred were changed boys. The old dominant faults I have told of had now to fight for sway and were generally mastered, whilst the conduct of one to the other grew generous and considerate, and the two boys became and ever afterward remained close friends.

Chapter Nine.
Big Fishing—A Strange Dissection.

The dog-days and the sultriness of August extended some of their influence even in our fresh kingdom by the sea. The only exercise that tempted us was swimming, and that, by Captain Mugford's permission, we now enjoyed twice each day—before breakfast and after tea. What else is so delightful and health-giving? The header from the brown rock from whose sides wave the cool, green tresses of the sea! off, with a whoop, and hands above your head, as the sun pats tricklingly your back! off, with a spring, down head first through the deliciously cool, clear, bracing water, that effervesces about you in bubbles of sport. Then, as the long delicate tendrils beneath swing like sirens' arms to welcome you, to arch the back and, leaving the alluring depths, rise through the dark water with the ease of an eagle on his wings until your head pops into the upper world of noise and sunlight again. The long, sharp, regular strokes now, every muscle stretching elastically and the whole frame electric with vigour and freshness—oh, how delicious!

Reeking with wet, we climb the rock, picking a spot where limpets are not, and sit in that glorious sunlight, each atom of which seems to melt into the blood. Clasping our hands about our knees, we can watch the glory of the sun climbing higher and higher above the ocean, and, if we choose, fancy ourselves big grapes ripening on "Lusitanian summers," until we are dry—which is too soon—and then with what overflowing spirits and ravenous appetites we go, like hunters, to the house!

"Come, Marm Juno, send in the eggs and bacon. We're as hungry as bears!"

"He! he! he! How you yun' gemmen do go on. Seems as ef you'se nebber git nuffen ter eat at hum. 'Spects you'll git fat down 'ere! He! he!"

But our studies did not slacken because of the warm weather. Copying Mr Clare, we all worked with a will. There was not a laggard amongst us, I believe. There was a disposition to please one who had so grown in our affection and respect as even to have outstripped our dear old salt tute. He understood our youthful difficulties, sympathised with our interests, and, not limiting his duties to hearing us recite, taught us how to study.

As August waned the fishing improved, and with the little fiddler or soldier crab we caught fish of three and four pounds instead of those of one and two pounds that had a month ago employed us. And then the striped bass, the Labrus lineatus, the king of saltwater game fish—what splendid sport they furnished!

These last we caught, some of us with the pole and reel, some with the hand-line. But it was active work to throw out about sixty yards of line and then troll it quickly back through the eddies off the rocks, where the bass fed and sported. The Captain was great at this; despising the pole and waving the bait round and round his head, he would throw it full a hundred yards to sea.

I tell you it was exciting to hook a five or six pounder and have him make off with a lurch. Pay out then, quick, quick, just keeping a "feel" of the fellow's mouth, and as he slacks his speed, tauten your line, and pull in with all your strength. Slower now, as he begins to haul back. Now look out; he is off again with a mightier spring and greater speed than before. Pay out, quick and steady. So, again and again, his strength getting less and less, until you can tow him up to the rock, and your companion put the gaff in his ruddy gills.

Many a noble fish escaped; many a line and hook snapped in the warfare. Sometimes a much larger fish would take hold, and two of us would have to pull on the line stretched like wire. During the season we took a seven-pounder, one of eight, and one of ten pounds, and Captain Mugford, alone on the rocks, one stormy morning, when we boys were in school, captured a royal fellow of twelve pounds, and brought it for our admiring gaze as we went to dinner. Mr Clare promised to beat that, but he never did.

One Saturday afternoon, about the last of August, just after a somewhat heavy gale, which had been blowing for a couple of days, we all repaired to Bass Rocks, though the sky was drizzling yet, and the spray of the waves dashed at every blow clear over our stand.

It was apparently a splendid time for our friends, the labrus, but we did not get a bite. We persevered, however, fresh baiting the hooks, and throwing out again and again, with not a fin to flash after them through the curdled waters.

Harry Higginson, having been very unlucky before this, losing several strong lines, had provided himself this time with one which, he said, could hold a hundred-pounder—the line consisting of two thick flaxen lines plaited together. He had it rigged on his pole. Grown careless from the ill-luck we had met, he at length let his bait sink to the bottom, about thirty yards from the rocks, and got talking with the Captain, who had given up fishing, and, with his sou'wester pulled about his ears, was taking a comfortable pipe in a crevice of the biggest rock.

Suddenly I heard a reel go clork—cle–erk cleerk! and saw Harry's pole fall from his hands to the rock. He seized it in a second, but as he stopped the revolving of the reel, the pole bent, and he pulled back on it—Snap! It was gone in the middle of the second joint. Of course the line remained, and that he commenced pulling in, bestowing the while some pretty hard expressions on his bad luck, for it really seemed as if the once-hooked fish had gone off in safety. About ten yards of the line came in slack, and then it stopped.

"Fast to a rock! What luck!" cried Harry, and then he commenced to jerk.

As he turned to look at us, with an expression of sarcastic indifference, I saw the line straightening out again in a steady, slow way, as if it was attached to an invisible canal-boat.

"Hold fast," I cried; "look! you have got something. What can it be?" saying which, Harry commenced to pull, but in vain—the prey went ahead.

Captain Mugford had taken the pipe from his mouth as his attention was fastened by the strange manoeuvres of Harry's game. Things having come to such a bewildering pass, he put up his pipe and, shaking the folds of the sou'wester from about his head, sprung forward and took hold of the line with Harry, but it still ran out through their hands.

"Seventeen seventy-six! what a whopper," exclaimed the Captain. "We must let go another anchor—eh, Harry?"

"Indeed! yes," replied Harry. "Look! he is stopping, and seems to be shaking the hook as a cat would a mouse. What can it be?"

Now the unknown took a tack towards us, and the line was gathered in and kept tight, and, as he began to go about on another course, his enemies took advantage of his momentary sluggishness to haul with considerable effect on the line. That brought the rascal right under the rocks. We could not see him; only the commotion of the water. Being brought up with such a short turn maddened the fellow, and perhaps he began to realise what was giving him such a jaw-ache. At any rate, just then he showed his speed to the whole length of the line, rushing off like a locomotive, and cutting his enemies fingers to the bones. They held on, however, and were able to bring him to as his charge slackened.

Of course the others of us hauled in our lines and watched with eagerness the combat so exciting. We proffered advice of all kinds to the two fishers, which they did not heed but devised schemes as the moment required, and certainly they managed with great skill. You would have thought the Captain was on deck in a hurricane, or repelling the boarders of a Malay pirate. The pipe was jammed up to its bowl in the side of his mouth, and all he said came in jerks through his teeth.

We were perfectly in the dark as to what the fish might be—whether an immense cod or halibut, or a princely bass.

The fight went on for half an hour without any decided result. But after that the struggles of the fish occupied a smaller space, never taking more than half the line out now. He was nearer the surface too, and the quick slaps of a tremendous tail lashed the sea.

"Mr Clare," called out Captain Mugford, "won't you twist two of the boys' lines together and bend them on that gaff? By the way, there is a hatchet with us, is there not? Good! Have that and the gaff ready. We are tiring the animal, whatever it is—a shark, I suspect."

Whilst we were carrying out the Captain's orders, Harry cried, "See, see! there is the whole length of him. Yes, a shark. What a grand beast!"

They were tiring him—worrying the strength and fierceness out of him. Every turn was bringing him nearer the rock. Every dash of his was weaker. But it must have been fully an hour from the first rush he made before he was brought exhausted alongside of the rocks, and the Captain cried, "Put in the gaff, Mr Clare—hard deep!"

Well was it that a strong line had been made fast to the gaff, for as its big hook struck him behind the gills, he uttered a sound like the moan of a child, and flapped off, the gaff remaining in him, into deep water.

With the two lines and his exhausted state, it was comparatively easy to bring him to the rocks again, and then with blows of the hatchet we had soon murdered him. Even then it was a job of some moment to get the body safely up the slimy and uneven rocks.

At length our prey was well secured, and we stood about him in triumph. It was a shark, measuring five feet and three inches in length, and he must certainly have weighed nearly a hundred pounds.

From the study Mr Clare made of the subject, we found that the name by which the shark is technically known is Squalidae, which includes a large family fitly designated, as your Latin dictionary will prove when you find the adjective squalidus—"filthy, slovenly, loathsome." It is a family of many species, there being some thirty or forty cousins; and the different forms of the teeth, snout, mouth, lips, and tail-fins, the existence or absence of eyelids, spiracles, (those are the apertures by which the water taken in for respiration is thrown out again), the situation of the different fins, etcetera, distinguish the different divisions of the common family. The cousin who, wandering about that stormy Saturday, had frightened away the bass, and finally astonished himself by swallowing a fish-hook when he only thought to suck a dainty bit of his family's favourite delicacy, was known as the Zygaena—so Mr Clare introduced him to us when his sharkship had grown so exceedingly diffident as not to be able to say one word for himself—a genus distinguished by having the sides of the head greatly prolonged in a horizontal direction, from which circumstance they are commonly known as the hammer-headed sharks.

His teeth were in three rows, the points of the teeth being directed towards the corners of the mouth. The two back rows were bent down, and only intended, Mr Clare told us, to replace the foremost when injured. These horrible teeth were notched like a saw.

I think the face, if so you might call it, of that piratical fish wore the most fearfully cruel and rapacious expression I had ever seen. That Zygaena family of the Squalidae, (I think they sound more horribly devilish when called by their classical titles), is one dangerous to man, and it is very rare that a man-eating or man-biting shark is ever found on the English coast.

I proposed to cut him open, and so we did. Among the half-digested food, most of which was fish, I found something that at first looked like a leather strap. I seized it and pulled it out. Surely there was a buckle. I washed and laid it out on the rock, while we all gathered about in great excitement to make out what our dead enemy had been preying on. There was no longer a doubt that it was a dog-collar—the collar of a medium-sized dog, perhaps a spaniel or terrier. There was a plate on it, which, with a little rubbing, we made to read, "David Atherton, Newcastle." How very strange! Had the little fellow been washed overboard from some vessel? or had he swum off some neighbouring beach to bring a stick for his master?

We could never discover any antecedents of any kind whatever to that mysterious sequel to "The Romance of the Poor Young Dog." Was there a fond master mourning for him in Newcastle, England, or in Newcastle, Pennsylvania? Alas, poor dog! thou wert hastily snatched from this world— the ocean thy grave and a shark's belly thy coffin. Thy collar hangs, as I write this, over my study table, and many a time has my old Ponto sniffed at that relic of a fellow-dog, and his eyes grown moist as I repeated to him my surmises of the sad fate of David Atherton's companion.

Mr Clare told us a good deal about sharks. Of the many varieties, the most hideous is the Wolf-fish, (Anarrhicas lupus). Though much smaller than the white shark, he is a very formidable creature. He has six rows of grinders in each jaw, excellently adapted for bruising the crabs, lobsters, scallops, and large whelks, which the voracious animal grinds to pieces, and swallows along with the shells. When caught, it fastens with indiscriminate rage upon anything within its reach, fights desperately, even when out of the water, and inflicts severe wounds if not avoided cautiously. Schönfeld relates this wolf-fish will seize on an anchor and leave the marks of its teeth in it, and Steller mentions one on the coast of Kamschatka, which he saw lay hold of a cutlass, with which a man was attempting to kill it, and break it to bits as if it had been made of glass. This monster is, from its great size, one of the most formidable denizens of the ocean; in the British waters it attains the length of six or seven feet, and is said to be much larger in the more Northern seas. It usually frequents the deep parts of the sea, but comes among the marine plants of the coast in spring, to deposit its spawn. It swims rather slowly, and glides along with somewhat of the motion of an eel.

The white shark is far more dreadful, from its gigantic size and strength; its jaws are also furnished with from three to six rows of strong, flat, triangular, sharp-pointed, and finely serrated teeth, which it can raise or depress at will.

This brute grows to a length of thirty feet, and its strength may be imagined from the fact that a young shark, only six feet long, has been known to break a man's leg by a stroke of its tail. Therefore, when sailors have caught a shark at sea, with a baited hook, the first thing they do when it is drawn upon deck is to chop off its tail, to prevent the mischief to be dreaded from its immense strength.

Hughes, the author of the "Natural History of Barbadoes," relates an anecdote which gives a good idea of the nature of this monster: "In the reign of Queen Anne a merchant ship from England arrived at Barbadoes; some of the crew, ignorant of the danger of doing so, were bathing in the sea, when a large shark suddenly appeared swimming directly towards them. All hurried on board, and escaped, except one unfortunate fellow, who was bit in two by the shark. A comrade and friend of the man, seeing the severed body of his companion, vowed instant revenge. The voracious shark was seen swimming about in search of the rest of his prey, when the brave lad leaped into the water. He carried in his hand a long, sharp-pointed knife, and the fierce monster pushed furiously towards him. Already he had turned over, and opened his huge, deadly jaws, when the youth, diving cleverly, seized the shark somewhere near the fins with his left hand, and stabbed him several times in the belly. The creature, mad with pain and streaming with blood, attempted vainly to escape. The crews of the ships near saw that the fight was over, but knew not which was slain, till, as the shark became exhausted, he rose nearer the shore, and the gallant assailant still continuing his efforts, was able, with assistance, to drag him on shore. There he ripped open the stomach of the shark and took from it the half of his friend's body, which he then buried together with the trunk half."

The negroes are admirable swimmers and divers, and they sometimes attack and vanquish the terrible shark, but great skill is necessary.

When Sir Brooke Watson, as a youth, was in the West Indies, he was once swimming near a ship when he saw a shark making towards him. He cried out in terror for help, and caught a rope thrown to him; but even as the men were drawing him up the side of the vessel, the monster darted after, and took off his leg at a single snap.

Fortunately for sea-bathers on our shores, the white shark and the monstrous hammer-headed zygaena seldom appear in the colder latitudes, though both have occasionally been seen on the British coasts.

The northern ocean has its peculiar sharks, but some are good-natured, like the huge basking shark, (S maximus), and feed on seaweeds and medusae and the rest, such as the picked dog-fish, (Galeus acanthius), are, although fierce, of too small a size to be dangerous to man.

But the dog-fish and others, such as the blue shark, are very troublesome and injurious to the fisherman; though they do not venture to attack him, for they hover about his boat and cut the hooks from his lines. Indeed, this sometimes leads to their own destruction; and when their teeth do not deliver them from their difficulty, the blue sharks, which hover about the coast of Cornwall during the pilchard season, roll their bodies round so as to twine the line about them in its whole length, and often in such a way that Mr Yarrell has known a fisherman give up as hopeless the attempt to unroll it.

This shark is very dangerous to the pilchard drift-net, and very often will pass along the whole length of net, cutting out, as if with shears, the fish and the net which holds them, and swallowing both together.

Chapter Ten.
Ugly—Plover, Snipe, and Rabbit Shooting—A Cruise Proposed.

Recounting that last event reminds me of a well-beloved character in our cape days—one, too, that was destined to play an important part in our little drama.

Ugly was his name; Trusty Greatheart it should have been.

Ugly was a clipped-eared, setter-tailed, short-legged, long-haired, black-nosed, bright-eyed little mongrel. In limiting his ancestry to no particular aristocratic family, he could prove some of the blood of many. There were evident traces of the water-spaniel, the Skye terrier, and that most beautiful of all the hound family—the beagle.

I do not know what education Ugly may have had in his earlier days, but I believe it to have been limited, though his acquirements were great. I believe him to have been a canine genius. He was as ready on the water as on the land. His feats of diving and swimming were remarkable; and a better rabbit-dog and more sagacious, courageous watchdog never lived. As to the languages, I will acknowledge he could speak none; but he understood English perfectly, and never failed to construe rightly any of Mr Clare's Latin addresses—much better than ever Walter could do. Indeed, Mr Clare's commands to and conversations with Ugly were always in Latin.

Of his rare sagacity and unbounded affection there are proofs to be furnished further on in this narrative.

Harry Higginson and Walter had guns, and they alone of our number were allowed to use them. That exclusion never caused me any regrets, nor do I think it troubled Alfred Higginson, but it was a constant pain to Drake. He loved a gun, and his most golden dream of manhood's happiness was the possession of a good fowling-piece. The prohibition of our parents, however, was so stringent in this particular that poor Drake never sighted along the bright barrels nor even touched the well-oiled stocks but once while we were at the cape.

There they stood, always ready, in a corner of our attic—where Drake, Alf, and I could not touch them, but ready at any time for the pleasure of Walter and Harry.

Walter was an accomplished shot, and Harry was not a bad one. Harry had not had the training of Walter, whom my father had taught—not commencing with stationary objects, but with targets thrown in the air, and small, slow-winged birds as they flitted near the ground. My father had at first made him practise for a long time without caps, powder, or shot, merely in quickly bringing the stock close to the shoulder, and getting the eye directly behind the breech. When proficiency in that had become a mechanical habit, the gun was loaded, and then commenced the practice of shooting at moving objects. As the art of bringing the gun properly to the cheek had been so thoroughly mastered as to require no effort nor attention, Walter could, when an object was thrown up, direct all his care to bringing the muzzle of the piece—the sight—directly on that object. My father's reason for teaching him first to shoot at flying marks was to prevent the habit of dwelling long on an aim—that habit of following or poking at the bird which ruins good shooting, and prevents the possibility of becoming a good snap shot. And so, afterwards, Drake and I were taught; and boys who are learning to shoot will find, that by remembering and practising the method I have described, instead of commencing by taking long, deliberate aims at stationary objects, they will get ahead surprisingly fast, far outstripping those who learn by the latter way.

In our rambles about the cape, Ugly soon displayed his talent for rabbit-hunting. He would smell where Bunny had been wandering and follow the track until he started Miss Long-ears from her covert, and then the fun began—the rabbit leaping off in frightened haste, running for life, winding and dodging about over the swells of the sparse grass hillocks, while Ugly, mad with excitement, spread his long, low body down to the chase. How the little fellow would put in his nose close to the ground, staunch on the trail as the best-blooded hound, and making the air ring with his sharp but musical bark! I tell you that was fun! Ugly always stuck to his game until he had run it to its burrow. He had not the speed to overtake it.

The summer is not the proper season for rabbit-shooting; so Walter, who was never to be tempted by the best chance of killing game even a day out of season, would not permit either Harry or himself to shoot at the objects of

Ugly's furious energy until it was legitimate. That conduct of Walter and Harry was beyond Ugly's comprehension. I have often seen him try to understand it. The chase having ended as usual in a safe burrow, I have noticed Ugly—who, after a very short experience, had learned not to waste his time in vain digging—turn toward us with a waddling, disconsolate trot, and having approached a few rods, stop and sit down to revolve the puzzle over in his mind. He would look where the rabbit had housed himself, then drop his head, cock up an ear, and cast an inquiring glance toward us, as much as to say: "Why, do tell Ugly why you did not shoot that old lap-ears? Ah!" That operation he would repeat several times before rejoining us, and when he had come up he would cock his head first one side and then the other, and look into our faces with most beseeching questioning in those great, keen, brown eyes of his. Then he would hang behind on our way home, evidently greatly distressed at his ignorance.

Never mind, good Ugly! I believe you were fully rewarded for weeks of bewilderment when the time did come for knocking over bunnies.

One afternoon, in returning from one of those rambles, we met our salt tute hurrying towards us in a great state of haste and perspiration. When near enough for his hoarse bass voice to reach us, he hailed—

"Well, there you are, boys, at last! I have been hunting for you all over the cape for the last hour. Ah! Ugly, boy, are you glad to see the old Captain trudging over the rabbit-ground? Eh? shaggy boy! And you have been running the bunnies till you are blown, and your masters would not shoot—eh? Well, no matter; the Captain shall bring his marline-spike along some day, and help you bag them. But, my affectionate pup, do you take a turn in that tail, or you'll wag it off some windy day."

So Ugly sat down—a long, red, wet tongue hanging from the side of his mouth —and whipped the grass between the Captain's boots with that restless tail until we came up.

"Why, Captain Mugford," said Walter, "I did not know you ever wanted us."

"No? Well, I do though, just now. You see, boys, as to-morrow will be Saturday, with every prospect of fair weather and a good breeze, I thought we might go on a cruise—start early, get our meals on board, run off to the fishing-grounds, and make a voyage of general exploration. And to do this we must get our traps aboard this evening, and see that everything is in order on board the Youth."

"Good! nothing could suit us better, Captain. I'll run to the house with the guns," said Harry, "and we can all go at once off to the Youth."

"Mr Clare," continued Captain Mugford, "can't go with us, he says, but must walk over to Q—town and spend the day. That's a pity, for I calculated on having a capital time all together, on a voyage like this one we propose."

"Well, we boys," said Walter, "will ask him this evening to put off his visit. Perhaps he may change his mind."

When Harry returned we went down to our cutter, all in great spirits on account of the fun proposed for the next day.

Getting on board, we mopped and swabbed her out well, overhauled the ropes and sails, and hauled down the pennant to take home with us for Juno to mend where it had frayed out on the point. That work being completed, we went to the house for such provisions as we should want on our excursion. Juno put up a large supply for one day—ground coffee, eggs, biscuit, cold mutton, a cold turkey, and several currant and apple pies, besides butter, salt, etcetera—and Clump conveyed it down to the Youth for us on a wheelbarrow.

The provisions were carefully stowed in the forepeak, and everything being arranged, we appointed Ugly to act as a guard over our craft during the night.

Harry briefly explained it to him. "Look here, Ugly, you are to stay here to-night and look after the things. Of course you are not to come ashore or leave duty for a minute. We shall be down early in the morning. Be ready to receive us with proper ceremonies, for we are off on a cruise, old boatswain, to-morrow. Look, Ugly; I put your supper in this stern locker. Do you see?"

Ugly was at first rather disappointed at the prospect of being separated from us for the night, but as Harry's harangue proceeded and he began to comprehend the honour of the duty required aboard ship, he bristled up and grew as stiff and important as his inches would allow. He turned his nose to watch where the supper was placed, and then walked forward and took a seat on the bow assuming a comical air of "captaincy;" so pantomimic was it that Captain Mugford laughed aloud, and said: "Well done, Ugly; where, my fine fellow, did you learn quarterdeck airs?"

"Good-night, Captain Ugly," we cried, as we pushed for the shore in the punt. "Good-night, boy; can't you say something, Captain Gruff?"

At which address Ugly rose up and, putting his forefeet on the larboard gunwale, barked three loud, clear notes, and we gave three laughing cheers as he returned to his post by the bowsprit.

Before going to bed that night, I went out in the kitchen to put a pair of my shoes to dry, and found Clump and Juno, as usual in the evenings, smoking and dozing over the fire.

Wondering at the amount of comfort these old folk seemed to find in tobacco, I asked Clump why he smoked so much.

"Fur constellation, Massa Bob—fur constellation; dat's ol," he answered.

"Oh, that is it, Clump—consolation, eh? Well, I must get a pipe some time and try it," I said.

"No, Massa Bob," joined in Juno, who was knocking out the ashes from her pipe on the head of the fire-dog—"no, Massa Bob you'se munno 'moke. 'Spects, ef you'se do, you find de way tur constollaton, dat ole Clump talk of, cum tru much tribble-laison—he! he! he!"

I had to laugh at the old woman's wit. As for Clump, he rubbed his shins and "yaw-ha'd" over his wife's speech for five minutes.

As I was going off to bed, Juno called me back in a hesitating way, and said in a low, frightened voice: "Massa Bob, sum-how dis ole woman ees 'feared 'bout ter'morrow. You'se gwine sure?"

"Of course, Juno," I replied. "And what are you afraid of? I would not stay at home for ten pounds."

"Dis chile's sorry—sorry," she continued, "but de Lor' ees my strong 'an my sheel." She was speaking very slowly, and had bent over the fire to rake the ashes together. She went on muttering some more of the Bible texts she always called on in any perplexity, until a new idea flashed to her from some uncovered ember, and she turned quickly, laughing in a low, shrill way, "He! he! he! woy'se ole Juno afeer'd? He! he! he! 'spects it on'y debbil dat has tole lies to dis poor ole nigger when she's 'sleep."

Chapter Eleven.
A Memorable Cruise commences.

We had nearly reached our cutter before the sun lifted its yellowish, red sphere, with just such an expression as a jolly, fat, old alderman accustomed to good cheer might present, on raising his head from the folds of a comfortable night's pillow.

It looked about in a dim, bewildered way at first, as if trying to wake up and make out what was the matter—that dark, vast, heaving, rolling sea, the rocks and capes touched with light, and a great land behind them yet dark and undefined; all so quiet too; and the soft, pink mist that rolled away in smoke-like clouds—rolled away over the billowy surface of the ocean toward the land, and, frightened, perhaps, by that red apparition on the eastern horizon, faded from sight, or rose for shelter to the sky above.

It was bravely up now; had mastered the situation, dispelled the night. The great honest face took a king's expression, and breathing bounty, warmth, and courage, blessed the scene it looked upon.

Then how the birds sang out, how sea and land grew beautiful and full of voice, how the clouds dressed their ranks and marched on their way. And the irrepressible exclamation came from all our boy lips at once, "How glorious!"

Ugly saluted us in a most vociferous manner, continuing his welcome from the time we left the shore to the moment we reached the yacht. "Behold," said Harry, "our rear-admiral waving his ta—I beg his honour's pardon—flag."

Yes—old Ugly kept his tail going in utmost delight, whilst he ran from one end to the other of the gunwale, assuring us that all was safe.

Sure enough, everything was in good order, but the supper had not been eaten. It had been pulled out of the after-cabin and inspected—that was all. Now Ugly's supper consisted of two things he could never be induced to eat—ham and cold potatoes; and Harry, from mischief—he knew, however, that the dog had had a hearty dinner—prepared those things purposely, supposing that Ugly's daintiness would fail in a twelve hours fast. But no; there the edibles were untouched.

"Come here, sir," said Harry to Ugly; "now why have you not eaten this nice meal, eh?"

Ugly's answer was merely to turn his head one side and look out at the sea, as if very much interested in something he saw—so much so as not to be able to attend to what Harry asked him.

"You dainty rascal, come along and eat this meal; it is good enough for any dog." And Harry put the despised victuals on another part of the deck, and, quite unintentionally, within a foot of the port scuppers. "Here, Ugly, eat it, sir, every bit of it."

Ugly's sensitive little spirit could not brook such a public mortification; but he was obedient in part. He approached the pieces slowly—in a dignified, contemptuous way—as he would have gone up to a cat, and, putting his nose to them, gave a push—away they flew into the sea.

Shouts of laughter greeted the act—Harry's the loudest—and he completed his attempt at discipline by calling to Ugly, "Come here, thou pluckiest and smartest of dogs. If you won't eat sailors' rations, come feast at the officers' mess on the luxuries of the fleet. How will that do, eh, old fellow?" cutting him off, as he spoke, a fat slice of mutton. "Another? well there! Bread and butter? Well, there is as much as you can eat;" and Ugly stowed it all away, triumph beaming in his eyes and wagging from his tail.

"Come, boys, now," said the Captain, "let's get under way. Cast loose the sails, Alfred and Bob. Drake, stand by to hoist the mainsail. Walter, take the helm. I want you to act as sailing-master this morning. Drake and I will get up the anchor. Is the mainsail ready for hoisting?"

"Aye, aye, sir," replied Drake.

"Then up with it. There—good!"

"Are your halliards all clear there, boys?"

"Aye, aye, sir," came from Alf and Bob.

"Hoist the jib, my hearties," cried the Captain, as the anchor came up. "Keep her head for the old church tower, Walter. There—steady, steady."

The Captain and Drake now secured the anchor, and the next order given was—

"Now, Alf, another pull on your main halliards. Get them well up. All right? Make fast."

The Captain lifted his hat and wiped with the bandanna his red forehead. Then he shook out a reef in his suspenders, and threw back his coat. "By golly! my hearties, we are snug now, ship and cargo; and what an air to breathe! I only wish this was a good ship of twelve hundred tons or so, Captain Mugford the skipper, and we were all bound for Calcutta together this splendid morning."

"Don't I—don't I," came from each of us in response.

"Now, my mates," called the Captain again, "we'll go about presently, when we get abreast of that tanned-sailed fishing-boat there off the port bow, and then, Walter, you can head her right out of the harbour. Let her go south-east-by-east, and we'll about fetch in ten miles as nice a bank for cod and halibut as there is off the coast. It is a small spot to get on nicely, and difficult to drop on often in just the right place; but it's no riddle to me, and if this breeze freshens a bit, as I think it will with the young flood, you can get out your lines in about one hour. So now let's have breakfast—the little rear-admiral, you know, had his long ago."

Yes—and the consequential Ugly was occupying a comfortable seat right under the jib, and only turned his head the least bit when he heard the Captain's mention of him.

"Keep her full now, Walter, ready to go about. Let go the jib-sheet, Bob; and now, down with your helm, Walter!"

The mainsail flapped twice. By that time the foresail had filled on the other tack. The cutter went about like a dancer on her heel, and we were off on the other tack, standing out of the harbour for the open sea ahead.

Then, the breakfast having been got out of the cuddy in the meanwhile, and arranged for our onset by Drake, we seized cups, knives and forks, and were soon very busy.

What a glorious thing to remember and marvel at, and wish back again, is a boy's appetite. And if any good old fellow is reading, who is not ashamed to recall those best of days—boyhood days—who is not ashamed to recall them, aye, with pride and smiles, let him think now of the suppers after Saturday tramps, of the Christmas and Michaelmas dinners, and of meals like that I am describing, when, after two hours in the early morning air, bowling along in our cutter, the sea-breeze swelling out our lungs as it did the sails, with merry hearts and perfect digestions, we found real fun—true animal happiness—in good bread and butter, a leg of cold mutton, and a cup of coffee. And to see the best of good skippers—as our dear old salt tute was—let himself down in a right angle after that on the deck, his back against the weather-side of the mast, and, heaving a sigh of vast internal satisfaction, draw out his pipe slowly, as if it was a ceremony too precious to be hurried, and, having put it just right in his lips and lighted it, puff the first long sweet wreaths of smoke; ah! that was a picture of creature happiness.

Chapter Twelve.
Good Sport—An Exciting Sail—Cast Away.

The absence of Mr Clare was the only drawback to our pleasure that morning. He had told us the evening before that he should probably return from his visit the same day, getting home about the time we expected to be back—about sundown, which at that date in September was at twenty minutes after six. He said, however, that possibly he might remain in Q—town until after Sunday morning service.

When Captain Mugford had completed his smoke, by which time we had a fine steady breeze from the south-east, he rose from his luxurious position and took Walter's place at the helm, saying—

"Not a permanent removal, Walter, but only until I can put the cutter just where I want her for fish. Fifteen minutes more will do that; so you had better go forward to Drake and get the anchor all ready to let go. You other boys can stand by the sails."

The Captain noted carefully the changing colour of the water as we drew over some bank, and he took bearings, too, from points on the land we had left nearly ten miles astern. In a few minutes he luffed a bit and sang out—

"Down with your foresail! Get in the jib."

The bowsprit pointed right in the wind's eye, and the boom hung fore and aft, the sail empty, as the cutter lost her headway.

"Is that anchor ready?"

"Aye, aye, sir!" replied Walter and Drake.

"Let go! About five fathoms, is it?" called the Captain.

"About that!" the boys answered.

"That's just what we want. Make fast! Now stow the mainsail, so that it won't be in the way of your lines, and fish. There, that will do! Now, all to the lines! Who'll have the first fish?"

In a minute Drake hauled that up—a cod—and the fun commenced. Cod and bass, and now and then a halibut, as fast as we could bait and pull! There was soon a lively flopping in our craft, and now and then a dog-fish would take hold, much to our annoyance, for generally he broke the hook or line, or else, if we got him in, made such a furious lashing about our legs that we had to finish him with a hatchet.

We lay at anchor there until we had had fishing enough. About two o'clock we stopped, having caught, as near as the Captain could estimate, between one and two hundred pounds of cod, a dog-fish, and eleven sea-bass—not the striped bass, such as we took off the rocks with a troll line in rough water: that was the Labrax lineatus; but the sea-bass, the Centropristes nigricans, superior in title, but inferior in every other way to the striped bass.

It was a job to pitch the fish together and out of the way, and then clean the blood, slime, and wet from our deck and get ready for making sail; but after some work it was done, and our lines stowed away.

"Now, boys," said the Captain, "we will have dinner, and get under way again. As the wind has hauled around to the east, we will take our course for the north. I want to show you that shore, it is so bold and wild. With such a stiff wind I reckon we can run up ten miles nearly, and then turn about and get home easily before dark. I say, boys, won't Mr Clare wish he had had a hand in catching that haul?"

Having finished the cold dinner with such an appetite as pleasure, exercise, and sea air give, we made sail and stood to the northward. The breeze was so fresh before long that the Captain told us to take a reef in our mainsail. Walter held the helm, and in little more than an hour we were sailing near the grand rugged shore that Captain Mugford had wished us to see. Here and there, in little coves defended by rocky sides, were the cottages of fishermen, and then great headlands of cavernous stone dashed by the waves. Again the shore fell to a lower level, and pines and other trees clustered together to defy the storms, and give pleasure to the eye. Farther on, the roughness of the coast vanished for a few hundred yards to make place for a yellow sandy beach where was stretched a long seine. Opposite that piece of strand, and close by our cutter's course stood a small stony island, bearing a single invalid old pine, from whose topmost branch a great bald eagle rose and hovered over our craft. Then the shore grew again like an impregnable fortification, and made out to a sharp cape, on the point of which stood a lonely, snow-white lighthouse.

"There, boys, we must go about now," said the Captain, as we neared the cape. "But see how the wind has fallen. If it holds on in this way we shan't have enough to take us home before night. Let's see what o'clock it is. That lighthouse is seventeen miles from the point of our own cape."

The Captain fumbled away at his waist-band—encircling a rotundity like that described of Saint Nicholas—and pulled out his immense gold turnip.

"Columbus' compass! Twenty minutes to five! Come, Walter, haul in the mainsheet, and come up to the wind. Are you ready to go about? Well, down with the helm then. I'll tend the jib. Those boys are so busy examining the fish that we will not interrupt them."

"No, sir," I said, "we are ready for anything."

"Oh no, Bob," replied the Captain, "go on with your studies. There is nothing to do just now. Walter, you may steer by the shore. But I don't like this slackening of the breeze, and it is drawing more to the south-west; we shall have it right ahead soon. The sun looks ugly, too. That murky red face foretells a row of some kind."

"I hope that we shall get the Youth safe at her moorings before night comes, or a storm either—shall we not?" asked Harry.

"We'll hope so," answered Captain Mugford, who pulled out his pipe and filled it hard, continuing, "Who'll hand me out a light from the cuddy?" I went in and struck one, and brought him a match, blazing famously. "Thank, you," he said. "Drake—just," (puff puff)—"just shake—oh! there goes that light!" I quickly brought him another—"just shake out—that—that—" (puff, puff). He had it all right now, the smoke coming in vast volumes; so he replaced his hat and removed the pipe from his teeth for a moment to complete the order—

"Drake, just shake that reef out of the mainsail."

"All right, sir!" said Drake. I helped him; but in half an hour the wind, as the Captain had foretold, was ahead, and not strong enough to fill the sails.

Fifteen or sixteen miles we were from home, with every indication that a heavy squall was to follow the calm settling down upon us. The dancing white caps of the morning had died away in a quiet, sullen sea, which only a land-swell moved. The sun had gone down to within a half-hour's distance of the horizon, shining on the distant western cliffs, whose variety, boldness, and ruggedness were magnified in outline and intensified in colouring by the heavy, yellowish-red glare which fell on them, and the sun's rays shot out in long forks, piercing the dark blue of the sea at all points in the western semicircle of our view. The atmosphere had grown warm—very warm for a

September afternoon.

We boys felt something portentous in the scene. The Captain grew uncomfortable, too, no longer laughing heartily or joining in our talk. He kept his eyes on the sky, and smoked pipe after pipe.

Even Ugly ceased napping beside Walter, and, uttering a whining yawn, as if sleepy but uneasy, walked forward to the idle foresail, and stood there with extended nose to smell out, if he could, what was wrong.

So we lay for nearly an hour, our only movement being with the outgoing tide, the sails flapping with the slow swell of the sea. But when the sun had disappeared the wind commenced to come, first in little puffs, now from one quarter and then from another. The gale would be on us in a moment.

The Captain took the helm then, and ordered us to stand by and be ready to tend the sails.

"Look out, too, for the swinging of that boom," he said, "and make Ugly get out of the way and lie down somewhere."

Ugly, hearing that speech, did not wait for further commands, but stowed himself away at the foot of the mast.

Now the wind came in heavier puffs, and then in squalls from the east.

"I hope it will settle there," spoke out the Captain. "It is coming heavier, but I hope steady."

He kept his eyes on all parts of the now lowering sky, and presently added—

"Take two reefs in the mainsail and shift the jib! Get the storm-jib up. Now hook on. Run it out. Hoist away."

That was done, no easy matter for novices in a heavy sea, and we flew away before the increasing gale. Fortunately the night was not very dark, there being a quarter moon to throw its light through the rifts of clouds.

How fast the sea got up! The wind grew heavier every moment. The mast of our little cutter creaked with each plunge, and the plunges were hard and quick. The scene was truly alarming, and we felt the danger of our situation. To be sure, we were comparatively safe if the gale should grow no worse; but it was increasing every moment in a manner that threatened in another hour to be too much for us. There was danger, too, that something might be carried away, or that, in the frothy sea and uncertain light, we might strike some of the sunken rocks that now and then stood off from shore like sentries. But the Youth leapt furiously onward from one mad wave to another, our good Captain steering with a strong hand.

The black, broken clouds rolled close to the sea, which seemed striving madly to swallow them; but on they flew with the screams of the wind. The thin moonlight, streaming unsteadily through the troops of clouds across the riven waves, had a ghastly effect—sometimes obscuring, sometimes exaggerating the terrors surrounding us. The shore, a mile to leeward, was to our sight only a bristling, indefinite terror; for there, where loomed the land we longed for, was the greatest peril—the line of fierce breakers that shouted their threats in terrible chorus.

I suppose we boys were all much terrified. I quailed with dread, for it was my first experience of a storm on the water, and its time and appearance were so imposing.

One would never have suspected from Captain Mugford's manner that we were in any danger. His face was as calm and his hand as steady as if we were having the pleasantest sail imaginable; only the violence with which he smoked, ramming fingers full of tobacco into his pipe every few minutes, betokened any unusual excitement, but we knew how absorbed he was in his charge by his silence.

We were speechless, too, holding on fast to the backstays or gunwale to keep our places in the desperate leaps and lurches the gallant little craft was making. Ugly was soon thrown from his station, and, finding he could not keep legs or position anywhere unaided, went and ensconced himself between our skipper's legs.

Harder, heavier blew the wind, and wilder grew the sea, so that it seemed sometimes as if we must go over, and the bowsprit now buried itself in every billow. Then the Captain said to us in a calm, steady voice—

"Boys, you must get another reef in the mainsail and lower the foresail. Now, be careful and steady about it. There is no hurry. Bob, you come here; the others can manage that work. You sit aft out of the way."

I did as directed; and the orders were speedily carried out without accident.

Boatswain's Half-Acre Reef, a low rock that stood out at sea, about three and a half miles south-east-by-east from our cape, now came in sight ahead of us to the windward. In the spectral light, and beaten on by the waves, it looked like some sea monster moving in the water. As we were going we should probably pass close to its lee side in about ten minutes, but the wind blew a tempest, and the sea increased so in a few minutes that our peril was terrible. For two hours we had battled—though evidently the storm was soon to be the conqueror.

Several seas came aboard in angry haste, and the punt, which had been in tow all day, broke loose and was carried away. Another sea, stronger than its fellows, suddenly struck us a tremendous blow. The cutter heeled over, so that the water boiled above the lee gunwale. The assaulting sea, too, broke up and over the weather-side, and drenched us all in its cataract. To increase our terror, a cry came from Alfred, who had been tossed from his hold and nearly cast overboard, but he caught the backstay as our yet unconquered boat rose from the blow like some brave but wounded animal. The water was several inches deep about our feet, and the good Youth had lost half its buoyancy.

Then came the Captain's voice again, steady and strong, but full of feeling—

"We'll get through it yet, lads, God protecting us," he sung out. "But all hands must try and do their duty. You know Nelson's last general order—'England expects that every man this day will do his duty.' That same motto carried out has saved many a stout ship and rich cargo, and the neglect of it has lost many more. Now, there's work for all of you. Walter, do you rig the pump, and Bob, do you help him, and the rest of you set to and bale. Be smart, now. There are two skids and a bucket, or use your hats. Anyhow, the boat must be cleared."

He spoke deliberately, not to alarm us, but at the same time we all saw that there was no time to be lost. Walter and I now got the pump to work, while the rest set to and baled away with might and main. I also joined them, using my hat as the Captain advised, for Walter could easily work the pump by himself. Still, in spite of the excellent steering of the old skipper, the seas came tumbling in over the bows and sides also so rapidly that it was hard work for us to keep the boat clear. Besides this, (notwithstanding her name, being an old boat), she strained so much that the seams opened and made her leak fearfully. It soon, indeed, became a question—and a very serious one—whether the boat could be kept afloat till we should reach our own harbour. We were now laying well up for the cape, though we were making what sailors call "very bad weather of it;" but, should the wind shift a little, and come more ahead, we might have a dead beat of several hours before us. We saw the skipper looking out anxiously at the reef I have described. A considerable portion, even at the highest tides, was several feet above water, and easily accessible. As the rock also afforded a shelter to numerous seafowl, which built their nests in its crevices, it would afford some security to a few human beings. Still, during a gale such as was now blowing, the sea washed tumultuously round the rock, and rendered the landing—even on the lee side—not only difficult but dangerous. I, for one, did not at all like the condition of the boat; still, as the skipper had hitherto said nothing, I did not like to propose that we should try to land on the reef. The old man was silent for some time; he again scanned the reef, and then he turned his eyes to the distant shore.

"Boys," he said at last, "I wish you not to be alarmed. The boat may very possibly keep above water till we reach the cape, if you can bale out the seas as fast as they wash in; but I am bound to tell you that there is a risk of our being swamped if we were to meet such a sea as I have seen, under like circumstances, come rolling in. There lies Boatswain's Reef—in five minutes we may be safe upon it—but much depends on your coolness and courage. The most difficult and dangerous movement will be the leaping on shore. Do you, Walter, make a rope fast round the bits; unreeve the fore halliards, they will suit best, and are new and strong. That will do; secure them well, and coil the rope carefully, so that it may run out free of everything. Now stand with the rope in your hand, and as I bring the boat up to the rock, do you leap out, and spring up to the upper part, where you will find a jagged point or more to which to make it fast. The rest of you, when the boat touches the rock, be ready to spring on shore; but remember, don't spring till I tell you. I'll call each of you by name, and the first on shore must stand by to help the others. There, I can't say more, except one word—be steady, and cool, and trust in God."

Walter did as directed, and we all stood watching the skipper's eye, that we might obey him directly he gave the word. It is a most important thing to have confidence in a commander. It is the great secret of England's success in most instances. Although there may be many shortcomings, both her soldiers and sailors know that, in nine cases out of ten, they will be well and bravely led, and the officers know also that they will be thoroughly supported by the men. If they go ahead, there will never be a want of men to follow them, even to the cannon's mouth.

On we dashed, amid the boiling, foaming seas. We had to continue pumping and baling as energetically as before. Had we ceased, but for half a minute, it seemed as if the boat would to a certainty go down, even before we could reach the rock. Captain Mugford did not address us again, but kept his eyes watching, now the heavy seas which came rolling up on the weather bow, and now the black rock towards which we were standing. All the time we kept carefully edging away, till we were under the lee of the reef—of that part, however, over which the sea broke with great force. Still, the water was smoother than it had been for some time. We stood on, continuing to bale.

Suddenly the Captain cried out, "Now, lads, to your feet, and be ready to spring on shore when I give the word." We all jumped up. Walter stepped forward and took the rope in his hand, as he had been directed. The Captain luffed up, and ran the boat alongside the rock; but there was still great way on her, and a tremendous crashing sound showed us that she had struck the rock below water. Walter sprang on shore, Drake and Harry followed, and as he leapt to the top of the rock, followed to help him make fast the rope round one of its roughest projections. Ugly sprang at the same time, and the rest of us went next—not a moment too soon. I was the last of the boys. The Captain came close behind me. He was securing another rope round the mast, and, with the end of it in his hand, he leapt on to the rock. As he left the deck, the boat seemed to glide from under him. "Haul, boys! haul! all together," he shouted. Our united efforts, aided by the surging water, got the fast sinking boat on to a rock. There the boat lay, little better than a wreck; but we were safe. We now saw how anxious our good skipper had been, for, taking off his hat, and looking up to heaven, he exclaimed, with a fervour I did not expect, "Thank God for His great mercy—they are all safe."

Chapter Thirteen.
Night on the Reef—Our Salt Tute's Sermon.

Our "salt tute" had gone through many a storm at sea; had once escaped, the only soul saved out of fifty-three, from a foundered bark, and endured five days' suffering, without bread or water, on a raft. But, as I heard him tell Mr Clare afterwards, he had never undergone an experience more painful than those two or three hours of gale in our little cutter. It was his affection for us boys; the reflection that he had proposed the pleasure sail, and the terrible sense of responsibility: those together had tried the old man's heart, head, and nerves, as they had never been tried before.

Among the exciting events of that night, one circumstance impressed me with astonishment, though it was but small matter perhaps for a boy to have noticed at such a time. It was that the Captain several times expressed himself in terms of piety, and even ejaculated that prayer when our safety was secured. We had sometimes heard him swear before that, and had always noticed, in contrast to Mr Clare, his indifference to any religious service or subject; indeed, the only emotion we had ever seen him display with regard to such matters was on the occasion of Mr Clare's address after the combat between Drake and Alfred.

It was eight o'clock when we landed on our little rocky island of deliverance. Boatswain's Reef was, as its name described, only half an acre in extent—a jagged, stony reef, raised but a few yards at its highest point above high-tide mark.

Very cold, somewhat anxious, and much exhausted, we found in a few moments the only shelter it afforded—a level place of sand and sea grass, about six yards square, defended on the south-west by a miniature cliff. There a lot of seaweed had accumulated, and the driftings of many gales collected. Several barrel staves, a large worm-eaten ship's knee, part of a vessel's stern, with all but the letters "Conq" obliterated, (the name had probably been Conqueror, conquered now, as Alfred observed, by old ocean); and many pieces and splinters of spar. The Captain made the discovery with us, and immediately suggested that we should shelter ourselves there and light a fire.

"Thanks, boys, to the necessities of my pipe, I always have a tinder-box in my pockets. Perhaps there are some not wet. Here, hunt for them; I'll throw off my pea-jacket, for I must go to work and try to save something from the poor

Youth—our grub at least. I want you to stay where you are, out of the storm, and to get a good fire going. It may possibly show them on the cape that we are safe."

"O Captain!" exclaimed Walter, "do let me help you. I don't want to sit here and do nothing but build a fire whilst you are at work and perhaps in danger."

"Come along, then, as you are the biggest and strongest—come along," replied the Captain, and away they hurried to where our good old boat was groaning on the beach and pounding against rocks with every beat of the sea.

She had been driven up too far to get off easily, but with a big hole in her bows it seemed probable that she would go to pieces before morning.

The sky was black everywhere. The roar of wind and waves was tremendous. The spray dashed in sheets, at every blow of the sea, over our spot of defence, so that it was difficult to start a fire. We were successful, though, and its light showed the figures of the Captain and Walter, by the stranded boat, climbing on board through the froth of the surf; pitched up and down as she tossed and bumped; getting down the tattered sail and hauling it ashore; jumping on the beach again with coils of rope; saving all that could be saved. And then, the tide having risen high, both together left her for the last time, bearing, at much risk, the anchor with them, which they fastened in a cleft of the rocks, that when our dear old boat—the home of many and many a fine time—did break up, something might be left of her.

We could not hear their voices, but saw the gestures for us to come and help, and in a few minutes we were all engaged carrying the rescued remnants up to our safe place.

Ugly helped. First he dragged a coil of rope and laid it beside the cliff; then he got hold of a loaf of bread which had dropped from among the other provisions, and carried that with some trouble but much pride.

In the storm and darkness, only fitfully broken by the firelight, we ate our supper under what shelter the low cliff afforded. Our boyish spirits were much subdued and awed by the peril we had passed through and the sombre scene about us.

The meal being finished, we made some preparations for the night, fastening the sail, by the weight of large stones laid on one edge of it, to the top of the rock, and then bringing its other edge, the boom side, to the ground and steadying it there with pegs. In that way we constructed a kind of tent, in which we piled a bedding and covering of dry seaweed.

The Captain stood by the fire, smoking his pipe and watching our arrangements. When they were completed, and we boys, gratified with our success, began to declare our situation "rather jolly," he interrupted us somewhat abruptly in this way:—

"You chaps always say your prayers before you sleep, I dare say. If so, you'll not forget them to-night—will you?"

"No, sir," we answered.

"Young shipmates, you remember how Mr Clare talked to you one day in the Clear the Track—eh? Well, then, for the first time in nigh forty years—think of that, nigh forty years—I said my prayers, the only ones I ever said, that my —mo—ther taught me; and somehow they came so clear to me that I felt like as if my—mo—ther was kneeling beside me. I ran away to sea, like the young fool that I was, when I was eleven years old. It was going on four years before I came back to my old home. I had forgotten my prayers. I tried hard to remember them, too, then, and some of the Scripture stories and lessons my—mo—ther used to teach me; for she was—gone."

His voice did not tremble, but he spoke very slowly, as if he wanted to speak out to us, and yet wished to do it without betraying the deep feeling that the events of the evening had intensified. Each time before he spoke the words "my mother," he took the pipe from his mouth and hesitated a moment, as if to steady himself. Somehow the old Captain's voice was softer, I thought, than I had ever heard it before—it may have been fatigue and the noises of the storm that made it sound so. His face, too, looked to me as if it had lost its hard lines and roughness—perhaps the firelight caused that to seem so. And those bold, sharp eyes of his were as gentle as my little sister Aggie's. He continued:—

"Hard times a youngster often has at sea, not in all ships, but in many, I tell you, and bad companions on every side. No gentle looks or kind words, but knocks and oaths. No time to read, and all that; hardly a chance to think. Well, I was a bad one, and worse when I went back again, and had my—mo—ther no longer to love me, and no one anywhere in the world to care a button for Rowly," (his Christian name was Roland). "I was a pretty reckless, hearty, devil-me-care fellow, I tell you. I could rough it and fight my way with the strongest, and never thought further ahead than the moment I was living in. So, for thirty years and more I knocked about the world, coming scot-free through a thousand dangers. Yes, and I got ahead all the time and prospered, thinking mighty well of myself, my good luck, clear head, and tough arm. I never thought of God. I don't know but that I had almost forgotten that there was a God; at any rate, if I thought of Him, it was with doubt and indifference. Yet, boys, in all that time, 'He cared for me, upheld me, blessed me.'"

His words grew hurried and thick, his head was turned so I could not see his face, and the old black pipe had fallen from his fingers to the ground. Ugly walked around and snuffed at it in amazement. But the Captain went on:—

"Now I feel it all—how I feel it—since I heard Mr Clare that day. Nearly forty years deaf, but I hear God's voice within me now, louder and louder every day; and what has He done for us to-day? How He has spoken! Ah! boys, you'll never be the old sinner I have been. 'Rememberthy Creator in the days of thy youth.' Part of the only hymn I can remember, of my mother's, has come again and again to my ear to-night—that—

"'God moves in a mysterious way,

His wonders to perform;

He plants His footsteps in the sea,

And rides upon the storm.'

"I forget the rest, except—

"'Trust Him for His grace:

Behind a frowning Providence

He hides a smiling face.'

"Boys! turn in now. I am on watch, and shall keep the fire going. Turn in, I tell you."

With those last words to finish his talk and order us to bed, his voice regained its sailor-like strength and roughness, but it melted again as he added—

"My dear old boys, we shall all pray to-night, eh? and from wiser and better hearts. Thank God!"

The last things I was conscious of that night were the whistling of the wind and the roaring of the waves, and the snapping and fizzing of the red embers, thus telling their stories to the storm of the brave ships of which they once formed parts.

Chapter Fourteen.
Ugly volunteers—Our Fresh Tute to the Rescue!

"Poor old Robinson Crusoe! poor old Robinson Crusoe!

They made him a coat of an old nanny-goat:

I wonder how they could do so!

  With a ring a ting tang, and a ring a ting tang,

Poor old Robinson Crusoe." Mother Goose.

The storm broke before morning, and a clear fresh September day opened on us castaways. There was no exertion of ours that could get us home, for our little cutter was a complete wreck, and we had but one of the many requisites for constructing a boat or raft—it consisted of the few planks and timbers of the wreck of the boat which still held together or had been washed upon the beach, and which, if we were not rescued before another morning, must be employed in feeding our fire. All the provisions we had taken with us on our day's voyage were consumed, except one loaf of bread and two pies, but a sufficient supply of the fish had been brought from the cutter to feed us for several meals. Of water—the greatest necessity—there was not a drop on Boatswain's Half-Acre. During the morning, the want of that became a pain, and before night any one of us would have given all he possessed for a single glass of cold water. Captain Mugford told us that now, for the fourth time in his life, he knew the suffering of thirst.

We must wait to be discovered, to be rescued, and before that we might die of thirst, for our island was only a low rock, and vessels going up and down channel kept generally too far from the reef to allow us to be seen by them on board. We could see our cape, and even the old house, but had no way of making signals, except by the fire at night.

Beautiful as was the day, it was one only of pain and anxiety to us. Of the few sails we saw, not one came within three miles of us. Where could Mr Clare be all this time?

The sea fell so fast that by two o'clock in the afternoon it was smooth as a lake. Harry Higginson and I sat looking at it on a point of the reef, with Ugly by our side. Ugly's tongue hung dry from his mouth, and he panted for a drop of water, but he was pained, too, I am sure, because of our silence and dejection. Watching our faces, as if wondering what he could do for us, he at length walked down to the waterline and looked across to the cape with a long whine. Then he ran back and put his paws on Harry's knee, as if he would have him say something. So Harry patted his head and said, "Yes, old boy, I wish we could get there."

He sprang down again and commenced to bark, pointing his nose towards the cape.

I called to him, "Don't be a fool, Ugly; your little bark can't reach them."

He cried and ran back to Harry, but in a second more, barking like fury, he ran to the water and swam off in the direction of our home.

We called to him again and again, entreating and commanding his return; but he paid no attention to us, and swam on. We were filled with sorrow and alarm, for surely little Ugly could not swim that distance—over three miles. We called to the Captain and the boys, and in a few minutes we were all standing watching the progress of brave Ugly.

What was going on at the cape all this time?

Mr Clare did not return on Saturday, and as night set in without our appearance, Clump and Juno got anxious. Having, however, great confidence in the Captain's care and skill, they were not so much alarmed as they might have been, supposing that he, seeing the approaching gale, had made some harbour, and that there we should stay until the weather changed. For some reason, both Clump and Juno supposed we had gone to the westward. That shore was broken by several bays and small rivers, and eleven miles westward was the fishing-village of —. Nevertheless, the good old people were somewhat alarmed, and sat up all night over their kitchen fire.

By ten o'clock of the next day their fears had grown too troublesome to allow further inaction. Clump pulled over in his punt to the village, across the bay. There he got some sailors to take a boat and go down the south coast to look for us, and gathering all the advice and surmises he could, (which were not consoling), from seafaring men he knew, returned to the cape.

When Juno heard Clump's report, her distress was very great. As she groaned, and wiped her wet, shrivelled eyes with a duster, she said—

"Lor' o' Marsy! Clump, ef harm's cum ter dem chiles ob Massa Tregellin—den—den—you berry me—berry dis ole 'ooman deep."

"Now, toff your mout, June—toff your mout! Wen I'se done berry you, ou yer 'spects gwine 'posit Clump en de bowels ob de arth, ay? He jist stay here and tink."—He did not mean think, but another word commencing with that unpronounceable s—"You'se fool, ole 'ooman; when you'se begin mittrut de Lor', ay?"

Clump was so frightened himself that he had to talk pretty strong to his spouse.

Mr Clare, after morning service in the church at Q—town, where he had gone to hear a college friend preach, took advantage of the lovely autumn day to walk home, which was about ten miles. He made his way slowly, enjoying every foot of the road, little contemplating the shock he was to receive at his journey's end.

He heard Clump and Juno's report without a word, only growing paler and paler. Then he sat down and covered his face, and, after a moment of silence, asked the negroes certain questions as to the course they supposed us to have taken, as to the storm on the cape, etcetera, etcetera.

He started off after that on a hard run for Bath Bay, where he jumped into a boat, and, pulling out into the greater bay, rowed with all his strength over to the village; but his inquiries there could gain no information, so he hired a small schooner-rigged boat and its owner to go out with him and hunt us up, or find some trace of our fate.

Mr Clare could not be still whilst the boatman, who had to go up to his home first, was getting ready, but ordered him to make all haste and call for him off the cape, and then he jumped into his own boat again and recrossed to the cape. But the boatman took a long time in coming, Mr Clare walking up and down the cape in the meanwhile, a prey to the gloomiest apprehensions. It was nearly five o'clock before Mr Clare saw his boat drawing near. At the same moment he heard a scampering through the short, dry grass behind him, and the wheezing of some animal breathing thick and quick. Turning, he saw, greatly to his surprise, Ugly coming towards him as fast as he could run. Poor little Ugly was dripping with water, and completely blown and tired out—so tired that, when he had reached Mr Clare's feet, he could only lie down there and pant. Mr Clare knew there was some important reason for Ugly's appearing in that manner, and though he did not suspect the exact state of the case, yet he lifted him in his arms and got on board the boat, which had now hauled in close to the rocks.

"Which way will're go, sir?" asked the grey, gruff boatman.

"Keep down south of the cape, near in shore. Clump says they went west," answered Mr Clare.

Poor Ugly had somewhat recovered by being wrapped up in Mr Clare's warm coat, and when he had put his nose into a pail of water that was on board, he kept it there until the bucket was empty, much to the surprise of both Mr Clare and Phil Grayson, the old boatman. Further strengthened and refreshed by something to eat, Ugly jumped up on the bow to see where they were going.

He showed evident signs of disapprobation when he saw the boat steering west; running to the stern, he there stretched his nose out to the east, and barked furiously. Mr Clare, thinking from the negroes' assertions that he must be on the right track, could not understand Ugly's uneasiness. How he had reached the cape, although it was evident he had been in the water somewhere, Mr Clare did not know, nor could he guess, of course, whence he had come. He only hoped that Ugly had left us in safety, and had come in some way to get assistance. It was nearly dark, and the wind had gone down with the sun.

Soon the boat lay becalmed. Ugly showed an unmistakable disposition to jump overboard, which, however, was partly quieted when he saw Mr Clare and old Phil use the oars; but when they persevered on the westerly course, Ugly, with an angry bark, sprang overboard and swam in an opposite direction. That movement proved to Mr Clare that they were going wrong, so the boat was turned and pulled in Ugly's wake until he was overhauled and taken on board. He shook himself, wagged his tail frantically, and kissed the hands of both Phil and Mr Clare. It was but slow progress with the oars against the ebb-tide. In about an hour, however, the first whiffs of the night-breeze came to fill the sails, and the oars were put in. They had rounded the cape, and old Phil asked again—

"Whar ne-e-ow, Capting—in shore, you think, or straight ahead?"

"Near the shore, I should think, just br—" but Mr Clare's reply was interrupted by Ugly's barking.

Skipper Phil put the boat's head to the north-east, to get nearer in shore as Mr Clare had said, and—splash! Ugly was overboard again and making for the east.

"You see, Phil," said Mr Clare, "you must get sailing-orders from Ugly, not me; and, Phil, I begin to be much encouraged by that dog's actions. He does not hesitate, but seems to have something important to do, and to feel confidence in his ability to do it."

"That's so, Capting," answered Phil, as, having got the boat about, he belayed the sheets and put the other hand to the helm; "he's a clever animal, he is. It seems to me that ar dog understands talk like a Christian. Did you take notice h-e-ow he was overboard as quick as you spoke, afore I started a shut? But whar are we going?—that's what I want to know."

"Phil," interrupted Mr Clare, "what light is that flaring up away ahead there on your lee bow?"

"By God, I see! the sails hid that—they did," Phil grumbled, and bent down to see beneath the sails. He chuckled some time before he answered, and his chuckle grew to a laugh. "Ha! ha! ha!—that ar light is on Boatswain's Reef, just as sure as my name is Phil Grayson. Mr Clare—hurrah!—your boys are safe."

Ugly, who had been lifted on board before that, joined his rejoicing bark to the skipper's merriment, and from the reef came a distant hallooing.

The flames at the reef grew brighter and higher. The sparks flashed and flew up to the dark sky. The shouting increased to yells. The rescuers on the schooner answered; and as for Ugly, the hero of our deliverance, he was almost frantic with delight.

The first words that were distinguishable from the reef were—

"Is that you, Mr Clare? Have you any water on board?"

"Yes!" was responded.

"Oh! do hurry, then—we can't stand this any longer!" cried out Harry.

In two hours more as happy a boatload as ever floated was springing before a fresh breeze toward the cape. Long before we touched shore our glad halloos had reached the old house, and lifted a heavy weight from the hearts of Clump and Juno.

They met us on the rocks, and each one of us had to undergo an embrace from their sable excellencies, ay, excellencies indeed, in devotion and uprightness such as this world seldom sees surpassed. Even Captain Mugford did not escape the ardour of the welcome; and whilst they hugged us the dear old negroes were crying like children, from joy.

Chapter Fifteen.
Evenings on the Wreck, with a Story from the Captain.

The favourite season of girls is, I think, Spring; and of boys, Autumn. One is the time of dreams, flowers, and emotions; the other, the period of hopes, courage, and accomplishment.

October, the fulness of Autumn, with its cool, clear, bracing air; with its gathered crops, rustling leaves, and golden light: October, when days of furious storm are succeeded by weeks of hazy sunshine and muffled quiet; when the fish are fat but greedy; when quacking seafowl and game of every kind tempt the lovers of good sport—

Ah! that is the time for boys.

We fellows gulped it up as the hounds do their meat when distributed to them, for by the end of October we should finish our six months at the cape.

This dashed our cup of happiness with regret, as the falling leaves and low winds moaning of winter touch October with a tint of sadness. But in one case, as in the other, the spice of regret was just what gave zest to the enjoyment of our pleasure.

The days being so short, it got to be our habit to improve every one of our daylight hours, out of school, in the many sports which invited us, and to do our studying in the evenings. So every night, as soon as supper was finished, we repaired with Mr Clare to the schoolroom in the old brig. There would be a wood-fire crackling in the stove, and two shaded, bright lamps hanging over the tables.

We took up our studies, and Mr Clare sat by, ready to answer questions or give explanations. When not busied with us he smoked and chatted with Captain Mugford, or read the papers and magazines. Ugly had his place on a mat where he could hear and see all that was going on.

Generally, during some portion of the evening, the Captain spread out his great red bandanna on his knees, and took a loud-snoring nap. Every movement of our salt tute's was interpreted by some corresponding signal of the bandanna handkerchief. When perplexed, he wiped his forehead with it; when amused, it blew a merry peal on his nose; in moments of excitement or delight, it was snapped by his side; when sleepy, he spread it on his lap; and once, I remember, he suddenly stowed it away—when much enraged by an impudent fellow who was shooting on our cape—in the stomach of his breeches instead of in the usual hind-pocket of his coat. The intruder seemed to understand the warlike signal, for he immediately stopped his insolence and made off. In fact, the Captain's red bandanna was like the Spanish woman's fan—a language in itself.

One evening we all finished our lessons early and drew our stools about the stove. Our salt tute was snoring bass and Ugly treble, so we did not disturb their dreams, but talked in low voices to Mr Clare, until, whether intentionally or irresistibly I know not, Drake gave a tremendous sneeze, so loud and shrill that Ugly sprang to his legs with a loud bark, and the Captain's head bounced from his chest and struck the back of his chair with a bang.

"Bless my heart!" said the Captain, clutching the handkerchief from his knees, and commencing to wipe his head with it. "Bless my soul, I rather think that I must have been napping. There you are, all laughing around the fire, whilst I have been dreaming of—well, never mind—days gone by—you may depend on that; but, Ugly, what were your dreams about, eh?"

"We should like to hear, though, something about those days gone by, Captain," said Mr Clare, suspecting that the worthy old seaman was in the vein for story-telling. "It is a long time since you have spun us a yarn, and the boys have been much wishing for one."

"Ay, that we have, Captain," we all sang out together; "we should like to hear something about those days gone by which you were dreaming of just now. We are sure from your countenance that there is something interesting; come, tell us all about it."

"You'll be disappointed, then. It's curious, and that is all I can say in its favour," answered the skipper; "I was thinking, or dreaming rather, of a circumstance which I haven't thought of for many a year that I can remember, which occurred during my first voyage. However, I'll undertake to tell it you if, when I've done, Mr Clare will spin you one of his yarns. He can spin one better than I can. Come, make him promise, and I will begin. If not, I'll shut up my mouth."

On this, of course, we all turned on our fresh water tutor and attacked him. "Come; Mr Clare, do promise us to give us one of your stories. Something about your life in America; you saw a good many curious things out there in the backwoods, which we should like to hear. Do promise us, now." Thus appealed to, Mr Clare gave the desired promise; and on this the skipper, blowing his nose with his red bandanna, which he afterwards placed across his knees, began what I will call:—

The Castaways.

A Tale of the Caribbean Sea.

"Land, ho! Land, ho!" was shouted one morning, soon after daybreak, from the mast-head. I was on my first voyage to the West Indies, in the good ship Banana.

"Where away?" asked the captain, whom the sound called out of his berth on deck.

"A little on the starboard bow," was the answer.

The ship was kept away towards the point indicated, while the captain, with his glass slung on his back, went aloft. The passengers, of whom I forgot to say we had several, and all the crew, were on the lookout, wondering what land it could be. We found, after the captain came below and had consulted his chart, that it was a little rock or key to the southward of Barbadoes.

"We'll get a nearer look at them, in case any poor fellows may have been cast away there. I have known the survivors of a ship's company remain on them for weeks together, and in some instances they have died of starvation before relief has reached them."

As we approached the rock all the glasses on board were directed towards it, to ascertain if there were signs of human beings there. The spot looked silent and deserted.

"If there are any poor fellows there, how eagerly they will watch our approach —how anxious they will be lest we should sail away without looking for them," I said to myself.

While these thoughts were passing through my mind, I heard the first mate say that he could make out something white on the shore, which he took for a tent or a boat's sail. As we drew nearer it became evident that there was a tent, but no human being was stirring that we could see. Nearer still a boat was observed, drawn up on the rocks. On further inspection she was discovered to be a complete wreck. Melancholy indeed was the spectacle which told so clearly its own story—how the shipwrecked mariners had been cast on the island in their boat—how they had gone on waiting for relief, and how at length famine had carried them off, one by one, till none remained. Still our captain was not a man to quit the spot after so cursory an inspection. The ship, having got under the lee of the land, was hove to, and a boat was lowered. Charley, another midshipman, or apprentice rather, and I formed part of her crew, while Mr Merton, our first officer, went in charge of her, accompanied by some of the passengers.

It was a long, low, coral-formed island, with a white beach—a very untempting spot for a habitation in that burning climate. When we landed, Mr Merton told us to accompany him, leaving two other men in the boat. We followed close after him, with the boat's stretchers in our hands, proceeding along the beach, for the tent we had seen was some little distance from where we had landed. We had got within a hundred yards of it, when suddenly part of it was thrown back, and out there rushed towards us two figures, whose frantic and threatening gestures made us start back with no little surprise, if not with some slight degree of apprehension. They were both tall, gaunt men, their hair was long and matted, their eyes were starting out of their heads, and their cheeks were hollow and shrivelled. They looked more like skeletons covered with parchment than human beings. Their clothes were in rags, and their large straw hats were in tatters, and, to increase their strange appearance, they had covered themselves with long streamers of dried seaweed, strings of shells, and wreaths of the feathers of wild birds. Each of them flourished in his hand a piece of timber—a rib, apparently, of a boat.

"Who are you, who dare to come and invade our territory?" exclaimed one, advancing before the other. "Away—away—away! We are monarchs and rulers here. This land is ours, won by our trusty swords and battle-axes. Away, I say! or meet the consequences of your temerity."

I was at first puzzled to know who the people could be, but our mate at once comprehended the true state of the case, and with great tact endeavoured to calm the strangers instead of irritating them, as many would have done.

"Don't be afraid that we are come to interfere with you, or to trespass on your territories, most mighty sovereigns, as you undoubtedly are," he answered, stopping short and holding up his hands. "Just hear what I have to say. Lower your weapons, and let us hoist a flag of truce."

"Granted, granted. Spoke like a sensible man, most worthy ambassadors," exclaimed the person who had hitherto not said anything. And both, lowering their clubs, stood still, gazing inquiringly at us. I had never before seen the effect of a few calm words, and a steady, determined look, in tranquillising the fury of madmen. Such were, undoubtedly, these unfortunate occupants of the island.

"Listen, then," continued Mr Merton. I had never before heard him say so much at a time. "You see yonder ship: she is bound on a far-distant trip, and on her way she called here on the chance of finding any one in distress who might need aid. Should no one require it, she will at once take her departure. Can you tell me if any people are residing on your island who may wish to leave it? At all events, you yourselves may have letters to send home. If you will at once get them ready, I will gladly be the bearer."

The two unfortunate maniacs looked at each other with a bewildered look. The idea of writing home, and not going themselves, seemed to strike them forcibly.

"Home!" cried one, in a deep, hollow voice. "Home! where is that?"

"Old England, I conclude," answered our mate. "You have many friends there who would be glad to see you—father, mother, sisters, wife and children; or perhaps one who has long, long been expecting you, and mourned for you, and wondered and wondered, till the heart grew sick, that you did not come—yet even now faithful, and believing against hope, fondly expects your return."

Mr Merton had been skilfully watching the effect of his remarks. They were most successful. He had touched a chord which had long ceased to vibrate. Again the two madmen looked inquiringly into each other's faces.

"Is it possible?" said one, touching his forehead. "Has all this been an hallucination?"

"Norton, I do not longer doubt it," answered the other. "We have conjured up many wild fancies, but the sight of that ship and the sound of a countryman's voice have dispelled them. We are ready to go with you, friend."

The person who had last spoken seemed at the first to be less mad than his companion.

"I am glad of your decision, gentlemen, and the sooner we get on board the better. But tell me, did you come here alone? Have you no companions?"

"Companions! Yes, we had. We frightened them away. They fled from us."

"Where are they now?" asked the mate.

"On the other side of the island," answered the least mad of the strangers. "They dare not approach us. Perhaps you may find them. They will gladly go away. While you search for them we will prepare for our departure."

"Very well, gentlemen, we will return for you," answered Mr Merton, in his usual calm tone. It had a wonderful effect in soothing the irritation of the madmen.

We took our way in the direction they pointed across the island. After walking and climbing some way over the uneven ground, we came in sight of a hut built of driftwood and pieces of wreck, almost hid from view in the sheltered nook of the rock. No one was moving about it. Its appearance was very sad and desolate.

"Perhaps the unfortunate people are all dead," remarked Charley to me. "I think, from what those two strange men down there said, they have not seen them for a long time."

We went on, apprehending the worst. As we got nearer, we hallooed to warn anybody who might be there of our coming, so as not to take them by surprise. Again we hallooed, and directly afterwards we saw the head of a man appear at an opening in the hut which served as a window, while he thrust out of it the muzzle of a musket.

"Hillo, mate! don't fire. We come as friends," shouted Mr Merton.

The musket was speedily withdrawn, and a man appeared at the door of the hut, followed closely by another. There they both stood, closely regarding us with looks of wonder. As they saw us they called to some one inside, and two more men appeared at the door of the hut, stretching out their hands towards us. Their clothes were in rags and tatters, and they had a very wretched, starved appearance.

"Are you come to take us from this?" inquired the man we had at first seen, in a hollow, cavernous voice.

"I hope so, if you wish to go," answered the mate.

"Go! yes, yes, at once—at once!" shouted the poor wretches, in the same hollow tones. "We thought at first you were two madmen who are living on the opposite side of the island."

Mr Merton told them that they need be no longer afraid of the madmen, and that as he had no time to remain, they must accompany him at once to the boat.

The first speaker, who said that he was the mate of the vessel to which the rest belonged, replied that he was afraid none of them would be able to walk across the island, as they had scarcely any strength remaining, and that he believed a few days more would have finished their miseries.

While Mr Merton and the mate were speaking, the rest beckoned us to come into the hut. Heaps of empty shells and bones of fish showed what had been for long their principal food. Some dried seaweed had served as their beds, and a tin saucepan appeared to have been their only cooking utensil, while a cask contained a very small supply of water.

From their appearance, I do not think that they could have existed many days longer. The only weapon they had was the musket which had been presented at our approach, but the mate confessed that they had not a grain of gunpowder, but that he thought by showing it he might frighten away the madmen, for whom he mistook us. They had, consequently, been unable to shoot any of the birds which frequented the rock, though they had collected some eggs, which had proved a valuable change in their diet. As time pressed, Mr Merton urged them to prepare for their departure. Having collected a few trifling articles, relics of their long imprisonment, they declared themselves ready to make the attempt to move. Charley and I helped along the mate, who was the strongest, while Mr Merton and the two seamen who had accompanied us assisted the other three. Even as it was, so weak were they, that without the utmost aid we could afford them they could not have crossed the island. They had frequently to sit down, and almost cried like children with the pain and fatigue they suffered.

Poor fellows! we had not stopped to ask any questions as to the particulars of their disaster, but as we went along the mate gave us some of the details. From the way he spoke, I saw that, though a very quiet, well-disposed young man, he was not one formed to command his fellow-men. He told us that his name was Jabez Brand.

"I was second mate of the North Star, a large brig, bound from Honduras to London. We had a crew of fifteen hands, all told. Several gentlemen also took their passage in the cabin. Among them were two brothers, Messrs Raymonds, fine, tall, handsome men. They had made their fortunes out in the West Indies, and were returning home, as they thought and said, to enjoy their wealth. How their money had been made I do not know, but it was said they were in no ways particular. Be that as it may, they had very pleasant manners, and were very open and free in their talk. One thing I remarked, that they seemed to think that they were going to be very great people with all their wealth, when they got home. Some of the other gentlemen, it seemed to me, fought rather shy of them, perhaps because, as it was said, they had supplied slave vessels with stores, or had had shares in them, which is not unlikely. The North Star was an old vessel, though, to look at her, you would not have supposed it, for she had been painted up and fitted out so as to look as good as new. She was not the first ship I have seen sent to sea which ought to have been sold for firewood. In our run out we had only had fine weather, so she was in no way tried. On this our return trip, we had not long left port when a heavy squall came suddenly off the land and carried away our mainmast, and, the wind continuing from the same quarter, we were unable to return. We had managed to rig a jury-mast and to continue our voyage, when another gale sprung up, and blowing with redoubled fury, the ship began to labour very much in the heavy sea which quickly got up. Still, for a couple of days after this gale began, there did not seem to be much cause for apprehension, though the ship was making more water than usual. However, on the evening of the third day, finding the pumps not sucking as they ought to have done, I went down into the hold, and then, to my dismay, I found that the water was already over the ground tier of casks. I went on deck, and quietly told the captain. He turned pale, for he knew too well what sort of a craft we were aboard. However, he did not show any further signs of alarm, but told the first mate to call all hands to man the pumps, while he sent me below to tell the passengers that they would be required to lend a hand. We had been driven about, now in one direction, now in another, but were some way to the northward of the equator. The wind was at this time, however, blowing strong from the north-east, and to let both our pumps work we were obliged to put the ship right before it.

"All hands worked with a will, for we knew that our lives depended on our exertions. Even the Messrs Raymonds set to; but while others were calm and collected, they were excited and evidently alarmed. I thought to myself what good will all their wealth be to them if the ship goes down? More than once I went below with a lantern to see if we were keeping the water under, but I saw too plainly that, in spite of all we were doing, it was gaining on us. We searched about to try and find out where the leak was, but we might as well have tried to stop the holes in a sieve. At midnight the water had risen halfway to the second tier of casks. Still all hands worked on, hoping that by sunrise a sail might appear to take us off. I saw too plainly that the ship was sinking, but it was very important to have light, that we might see how best to launch the boats. Day seemed very, very long in coming. The captain tried to cheer the people, but he must have known as well as any on board that perhaps none of us might live to see the sun rise over the waters.

"All that night we laboured without a moment's rest. Dawn came, and I went to the mast-head to learn if a sail was in sight. I scarcely expected to see one, yet I hoped against hope. Not a speck could I discover on the clearly-defined circle of the horizon. The old ship was now fast settling down, and the sea was making a complete breach over her. To enable the water to run off the decks and to allow us to launch the boats, we cut away the stanchions and bulwarks between the fore and main rigging. Such food and water as could be got at was then handed up on deck, ready to be placed in the boats. The crew did not wait the captain's orders to lower them. He seemed unwilling to abandon the ship till the last moment. There was a dinghy stowed in the longboat. While the men were getting it out a sea broke on board, and, dashing it against the spars, drove in the starboard bilge, and at the same time washed two of the poor fellows overboard. We then got the stores into the longboat. A warp was next passed over the port bow of the ship outside the fore-rigging, and then inboard again through the gangway, and secured to the bow of the boat, sufficient slack being left to allow her to go astern. However, just as we were launching the boat a sea struck her, and stove in two planks of the port bilge. I now thought that it was all up with us, for though there was the jollyboat, she could not carry half the number on board; still it was possible that we might get the planks back to their places and stop the leak; so, in spite of the accident to her, we managed by great exertions to launch her, and I, with some of the crew and passengers, jumped into her with buckets and began to bail her out. Happily, the carpenter was one of the party. Some blankets had been thrown into the boat, which he immediately thrust over the leak and stood on them, while he got ready a plank and some nails which he had brought with him. While he and I were working away the boat was shipping many seas, in consequence of the weight of the warp ahead; I sang out that we must have it shifted, and after a light rope had been hove to us and made fast, it was let go. Meantime the quarterboat was lowered and several men got into her, but their painter was too short, and before they had got their oars into her she broke adrift and dropped astern. The men in her lifted up their hands for help; the captain, who was still on deck, hove them an oar, and we hove another, but they missed both of them, and before long a sea struck the boat and turned her over. It was very sad, for we could give her no help. We, meantime, in the longboat, were not in a very much better condition, for we were shipping a great deal of water. The captain now ordered us to haul up the boat, that the people might get into her; but while we were so doing, the roughness of the sea causing a sudden jerk on the rope, it parted, and we dropped astern. Cries of despair rose from many of those on board when they saw what had occurred. We instantly got out our oars and endeavoured to pull up to the ship, but the quantity of water in her made all our efforts unavailing. To prevent the boat going down we were obliged to turn to and bail. Away we drifted, every moment, increasing our distance from the ship, and lessening our hope of being able to return. There stood our late companions on the poop of the sinking ship, some waving to us, some shouting and imploring us to return. Summoned by the captain, we saw that they then were endeavouring to form a raft. The thought that the lives of all on board depended mainly on our exertions stimulated us once more to attempt to pull up to them. We got out the oars, and while the landsmen bailed we pulled away till the stout ash-sticks almost broke. By shouts and gestures I encouraged the people; every muscle was stretched to the utmost—no one spared himself—but our strength could not contend with the fearful gale blowing in our teeth. The seas broke over us, and almost swamped the boat; still, if we could but hold our own, a lull might come before the ship went down. But vain were all our hopes; even while our eyes were fixed on the brig, her stern for an instant lifted up on a foam-crested sea, and then her bow, plunging downwards, never rose again. Most of those who remained on board were engulfed with the wreck, but a few, springing overboard before she sank, struck out towards us. It would, indeed, have required a strong swimmer to contend with that sea. One after another the heads of those who still floated disappeared beneath the foaming waves, till not one remained; the other boats also had disappeared, and we were left alone on the waste of waters. The instant the brig went down a cry arose from some in our boat, so piercing, so full of despair, that I thought that some relations or dear friends of one of those who had escaped had been lost in her; but on looking again I discovered that it had proceeded from the two brothers I have spoken of. They had lost what they had set their hearts on—what they valued more than relations and friends —their long-hoarded wealth. There they sat, the picture of blank despair. I knew that it would never do to let the people's minds rest on what had occurred, so I cheered them up as best I could, and told them that I thought we should very likely be able to reach some port or other in four or five days. On examining our stores, I found that with economy they might hold out for nearly two weeks, and before that time I hoped we might reach some civilised place. I was more concerned with the state of our boat. She was originally not a strong one, and, what with the injury she received when launched from the sinking ship, and the battering she had since got, she had become very leaky. The crew, severely taxed as their strength had been, behaved very well, but two of our passengers gave signs of becoming very troublesome. I did not suspect at the time that their minds were going. At first they were very much cast down, but then one of them roused up and began to talk very wildly, and at last the other took up the same strain, and off they went together. They insisted on taking command, and having twice as much food served out to them as others got. At one time they wanted the boat to be steered to the northward, declaring that we should have no difficulty in reaching England. I had to hide the compass from them, and at last they were pacified under the belief that we were going there. Each morning when they woke up they asked how much nearer they were to our native land. There were three other passengers—an old man, a lad, and an invalid gentleman. Consumption had already brought him near the grave, still he lasted longer than the other two. The young boy died first; fear had told on his strength; then the old man died. I could not tell exactly where we were. We were always on the lookout for land, or a sail to pick us up. One morning at daybreak the man who had taken my place at the helm roused us up with the cry of 'Land! land ahead!'

"'Old England—old England!' shouted the madmen, springing up and waving their hands.

"'My native land—my own loved home!' cried the invalid, sitting up as he awoke and gazing long and anxiously at the rock which rose out of the blue water before us.

"Drawing a deep sigh when he discovered his mistake, he sank back into his place. Soon afterwards, finding that he did not stir, I was about to raise him up. There was no need for my so doing. He had gone to that long home whence there is no return. Those who loved him on earth would see him no more. Some of the people were in a very weak and sad condition. They had been sick on board—scarcely fit for duty. I knew what the land was—the rock we are now on; but, barren as it is, I thought it would be better to recruit our strength on shore than to attempt to continue our course to the mainland in our present condition. I therefore steered for it, and was looking out for a secure spot where I might beach the boat, when the madmen, growing impatient, seized the tiller and ran her on shore, where she now lies. We were nearly swamped, and everything in the boat was wetted. She also was so much injured that she was totally unfit again to launch, and we had no means of repairing her. However, we set to work to make things as comfortable as we could, and the first thing I did was to erect a tent to shelter the sick men from the rays of the sun. Poor fellows, they did not long require it. Three of them very soon died. We had now only six survivors of those who had escaped from the foundering ship. We were all getting weaker and weaker, except the madmen, who seemed to be endowed with supernatural strength. One day I, with the three seamen who remained, went out to collect shellfish and birds' eggs. I carried the only musket we had saved, having dried some gunpowder which I had in a flask. We had come back with a supply; but as we approached the tent we saw the two madmen standing in front of it, flourishing pieces of wood and swearing that we should not enter it, and that they were the kings of the country. Some of our people wanted me to shoot them, but that, of course, I would not on any account do. I could not even say that our lives were threatened. I stopped and tried to reason with the poor men. At last they consented to give us up a saucepan and some of the provisions, and we, glad to be rid of their company, resolved to go to the other side of the island, and to build ourselves a hut from the driftwood which we had seen there in abundance. This we did, but we all have been growing weaker and weaker ever since, and had you not come to our rescue I do not think we should have held out much longer."

The mate finished his account—on which, from what he afterwards told me, I have somewhat enlarged—just as we got up to the tent. The unhappy madmen stood in front of it waiting for us. Though excited in their looks and wild in their conversation, they seemed perfectly prepared to accompany us. They looked with eyes askant at the mate and his three companions, but said nothing to them.

"Well, gentlemen, are you ready to proceed?" exclaimed Mr Brand as we got up to them.

"Certainly, noble mariners—certainly," answered one of them. "But stay, we have some freight to accompany us."

And, going into the tent, they dragged out a sea-chest, which appeared to be very heavy. The mate looked surprised, and when they were not looking he whispered to me that he did not believe that the chest contained anything of value. He, however, had not an opportunity of speaking to Mr Merton, who told them that as soon as he had seen the people into the boat he would come back and help them along with their chest. This reply satisfied them, and they sat themselves down composedly on the chest while we helped the other poor men into the boat. As soon as this was done, two of our crew were sent back to bring along the chest. Though strong men, they had no little difficulty in lifting it; but whether or not it was full of gold, no one could have watched over it more jealously than did the two madmen. It was very remarkable how completely they seemed inspired by the same spirit, and any phantasy which might enter the head of one was instantly adopted by the other.

"There's enough gold there to buy the Indies!" cried Ben Brown, a seaman, as he handed in the chest. "Take care we don't let it overboard, mates, or the gentlemen won't forgive us in a hurry."

"It is more than your lives are worth if you do so!" cried the madmen. "Be careful—be careful, now."

The boat was loaded, and we pulled away for the ship. Our captain seemed somewhat astonished at the extraordinary appearance of the people we brought on board. The mate and other men of the lost vessel were carefully handed up. They were not heavier than children, but the Messrs Raymonds would not leave the boat till they saw their chest hoisted up in safety. Their first care on reaching the deck was about it, and, going aft to the captain, they begged he would be very careful where it was stowed.

"Stay! Before these gentlemen lose sight of it let it be opened, that there may be no mistake about its contents," said Mr Merton.

"What, and expose all our hoarded wealth to the eyes of the avaricious crew!" they cried out vehemently. "We shall be robbed and murdered for the sake of it, and this chest will be sent where many others have gone—to the bottom of the sea."

"You are perfectly safe on board this ship, I trust, gentlemen," remarked our captain. "Is the chest secured with a key?"

"Whether or not, with our consent never shall it be opened!" exclaimed one of the brothers.

"Then remember I can in no way be answerable for what is found in it when it is opened," observed the captain.

What new idea came into the heads of the two brothers I do not know, but they instantly agreed that the chest should be opened.

"Call the carpenter," said our captain, who wanted to bring the matter to a conclusion, and who probably by this time had begun to suspect the sad condition of the two gentlemen.

Mr Pincott, the carpenter, and one of his mates came aft, and made short work in opening the mysterious chest. Those who claimed it as their property started back with looks of dismay. It was full to the brim of stones and sand and shells. Again and again they looked at it; they rubbed their eyes and brows; they clutched it frantically and examined it with intense eagerness; they plunged their hands deep down among the rubbish; it was long before they appeared able to convince themselves of the reality; over and over again they went through the same action. At last one of them, the most sane of the two, drew himself up, and, pointing to the chest, said in a deep, mournful voice—

"Captain, we have been the victims of a strange hallucination, it seems. We have not lost sight of that chest since we filled it. We thought that we had stored it with gold and precious stones. I know how it was. Hunger, anxiety, hardships, had turned our brains. We had lost all—all for which we had been so long toiling. We conjured up this phantasy as our consolation. Is it not so, Jacob?"

The other brother thus addressed shook his head and looked incredulous. Once more he applied himself to the examination of the chest. At last he got up, and looked long and fixedly at the other, as if to read the thoughts passing through his head.

"You are right, brother Simon," he said, after some time, in a deep, low, mournful voice; "it's dross—dross—all dross. What is it worse than what we have been working for? That's gone—all gone—let this go too—down—down to the bottom of the sea."

Again influenced by the same impulse, they dragged the chest to the side of the vessel, and with hurried gestures threw the contents with their hands over into the sea. It appeared as if they were trying which could heave overboard the greatest quantity in the shortest time. When they had emptied it, they lifted up the chest, and before any one could prevent them that also was cast into the sea.

"There perish all memorial of our folly!" exclaimed the one who was called Simon. "We shall have to begin the world anew. Captain, where do you propose landing us? The sooner we begin the work the better."

The captain told them that must depend on circumstances, but it was finally arranged that they were to be put on shore at Barbadoes, where, after a long conversation together, they expressed a wish to be landed. The scene was a very strange one; the rapid changes of ideas, the quickly succeeding impulses, and the extraordinary understanding between the two. We found, however, that they were twins, and had always lived together, so that they seemed to have but one mind in common.

I never met an officer who took so much interest in the apprentices—indeed, in all the men under him. He took occasion to speak to me and Charley of what had occurred.

"How utterly incapable of affording satisfaction is wealth unless honestly obtained and righteously employed!" he remarked. "We have also before us an example of the little reliance which can be placed on wealth. These two poor men have lost theirs and their minds at the same time. Their senses have been mercifully restored to them. It remains to be seen by what means they will attempt to regain their fortunes."

I cannot say that Mr Merton's remarks made any very deep impression on me or Charley at the time, though I trust they produced their fruit in after years. Every kindness was shown the two poor men on board, and, as far as I could judge, they appeared to have become perfectly sane. The same kindness was also shown the mate and the other rescued seamen of the lost brig. We landed the mate and seamen, as well as the two brothers, at Bridge Town, in the island of Barbadoes, but from that day to this I have never heard a word about them.

Harry Higginson, some time before the Captain's yarn concluded, got up from his seat and went to the side of our cabin schoolroom and stood there, looking through a dead-light which was open to ventilate the room. He had remembered that it was about the time of the moon's rising, and went to watch it come up. As our salt tute finished, Harry turned from his lookout, and, catching my eye, beckoned me to join him, and so I did. Coming beside him, Harry pointed and whispered—for the spell of the story still lingered over us, and no one seemed willing to break it roughly—

"What do you make of that, Bob?"

The big mellow moon was right before us, and, as one would say, about the height of a house, above the eastern horizon. Its light silvered a path on the sea to us—a path that was bounded on one side by the bold, dark rocks of the southern shore of the cape, and whose limit to our right was as undefined as the undulating waters it was lost in. Across the stretch of moonlight, and a half-mile from the wreck, I saw a lugger heading for a point that made the southern side of a snug little cove which afterwards got the name of "Smuggler's Cove." It was the sight of that boat at such a time coming towards the shore of our rough cape that caused Harry's question to me.

"Singular—very singular," I answered; "we must watch that craft."

Mr Clare called to us, "Boys, what are you whispering about over there?"

We wanted to keep watch quietly by ourselves, on the discovery which promised some interest, so we did not answer, and Walter at that moment called on Mr Clare for his story.

"Well," said Mr Clare, "I promised a story as the only way of getting Captain Mugford's. I bought a great deal cheaply, and must pay now. In common honesty, therefore, I am bound to commence my story. I am afraid that I cannot make it as interesting as Captain Mugford's, inasmuch as his was about the sea, while mine relates to the land. However, I will begin."

Chapter Sixteen.
Mr Clare's Story.

The year before I left Canada, in the fall, as the autumn is called there, I started with a number of other young men in our neighbourhood, the county town of C—, to go about seventy-five miles up the Ottawa, what is called lumbering. The winter work is cutting down the trees and getting them to the riverbank ready for the spring thaw, when they are gathered in rafts and floated down to a seaport. We went provided for six months' severe life in the snowbound forests. Almost every man, too, took his gun or rifle. The journey to the site of our winter's encampment was made on foot; our clothes, provision, stoves, and cooking utensils being loaded on an ox-cart that accompanied us, the oxen being necessary to haul the timber to the river, as our work extended back.

After a week's journey, we came to the spot selected for our winter's work, on a bend of the river, ten miles above where the M— joins the Ottawa. Of course it is an utterly wild region there, never trodden except by hunters, and away beyond the usual search of lumbermen. I do not know why my uncle, the lumber-boss of our expedition, went sixty miles beyond ordinary timber-cuttings. Perhaps it was to procure, on a special order, a remarkably fine choice of oak and pine, and that that spot had been marked by him in some hunting trip or Indian survey as producing the finest timber in the colony. It was grandly beautiful there, where a valley, running at a right angle to the river's course, spread out at the bank to a semicircle, containing a hundred acres and more of most magnificent trees—a vast forest city, inhabited by immense patriarchs, grey-bearded with moss. Their dignity and stateliness and venerable air were most impressive; and when they sang to the strong wind, chanting like the Druids of old, even I, who had so long lived in a country of forests, was filled with awe. And we, pigmies of twenty and thirty years, had invaded this sanctuary to slay its lords, who counted age by centuries, and had lived and reigned here before our forefathers first trode the continent. The quietude and hazy light of Indian summer floated through the aisles and arches of the solemn forest city as we first saw it—a leaf falling lazily now and then across the slanting beams of the setting sun—a startled caribou, on the discovery of our approach, hurrying from his favourite haunt with lofty strides. All else in the picture before us was silent and motionless. Our winter's home! Those lofty coverts to be levelled to a bare, stump-marked plane! The old vikings of the primeval forests, to be fashioned by the axe, to battle with the fury of the ocean, and reverberate with reports of hostile broadsides—to bear the flag of their country in peace and commerce, too, to far-distant lands—all as triumphantly as they had for ages wrestled only with the winds!

You laugh, Drake; and you are right, for I doubt if many of us thought then in that strain. No, there is not much sentiment among lumbermen, and as we regarded those mighty oaks and pines, it was principally with speculative calculation as to how many solid feet of prime timber "that 'ar thicket would yield."

The first task was that of building log-houses—two for our twenty hands. In each was an immense chimney-piece, a cooking-stove, and a bed stretching the width of the house on the floor, with a mattress of hemlock boughs. The rifles and shotguns hanging over the wide fireplace, and a long pine table and rustic benches, completed the furniture of our houses. The oxen and a company of hounds and mongrels had their quarters in a low log barn between the houses. Our supplies of fresh meat for the winter depended upon the good use of the firearms, and each week some one man of our number was detailed as hunter.

That winter of 1824 proved the coldest ever remembered in America, but the long mild autumn gave no threats of the season that was to succeed it. Before the first snow—which was, I remember, on November 20—our little forest colony was comfortably established, and a score of big trees laid stretched in the leaves.

In our company were many fine, intelligent young men—all taught somewhat, some tolerably well educated. None had been to college. I little thought at that time of becoming a scholar and a clergyman. They were frank, generous, honourable fellows—honest and brave, but perfectly ungodly and reckless of Heaven's displeasure or the life hereafter. After the day's labour, the evening was dissipated in card-playing, swearing, and hard drinking. Many a scene of riot and orgies did those log-walls witness. Such is generally the life in a lumber-camp: hard, wholesome labour in the day, loud revelling at night. The rough, adventurous life, with no home charm or female influence to refine or restrain, is probably the principal reason of such low practice of life in the lumberman's camp.

The worst character in our company—and he happened to be in the same house with me—was a man of twenty-eight years of age, the son of a French father and American mother, and whose mother's grandfather had been an Indian warrior of some renown in the early history of our province. In him were united the savageness of the red man, the gaiety of the Frenchman, and the shrewdness of the Yankee. He was a large, handsome, and immensely muscular man, with dark complexion, small straight features, quick black eyes, and long raven-coloured beard and hair that hung down to his shoulders. Utterly wicked and unprincipled as he was, his merriment, off-hand and daring, lent him a certain fascination and popularity among us. He was very witty, his laugh was rich and constant, he sang well, and played in a dashing way the violin. Every night he found some one to gamble with him. Every night he drank a pint of whisky, and kept the cabin in an uproar.

I greatly disliked this Guyon Vidocq; because he exerted a most baneful influence in our company, all of whom except the boss were younger than himself.

The best man of our number was John Bar, and a fine Christian, cheerful-hearted fellow he was. Although differing so widely from Guyon Vidocq, he, without any effort to do so, and indeed unconsciously, disputed the palm of popularity with him. He was an active, powerful man too, and though terribly pockmarked, had a most agreeable countenance. He could troll a pleasant stave, and loved, when off hunting or at work with his axe sometimes, to sing one of our C— Sunday hymns, and whenever there was a respectable party in the evening, instead of the usual rioting set, he would willingly give them "The Fireside at home," "Merrily row, the Boat row," or any of the good old-fashioned songs, pure and inspiriting. Not another of us was so cheerful and industrious as John Bar. Drinking, gambling, or swearing, he was never guilty of, and when the evening orgies commenced he generally spoke to me, and we went off together to visit at the other cabin, or, if they were as bad there, find a warm corner with our blankets in the log barn, and there chat away the hours until our companions had calmed down and turned into their bunks. John Bar was not a meddler, nor what is contemptuously called, in such reckless societies as ours was, "a preacher;" but as he was loyal to his country, and loyal to his parents, he was far more loyal to his God. It would madden any man to hear his mother's name profanely used; it made John Bar's heart sick —yes, and I have seen him tremble with rage—when the name of his Saviour was taken as an oath. Sometimes then, and at other times when the wickedness in camp was rampant, he would break out in words of fire—words of fire that soon mingled with, and at last wholly changed to, words of love and entreaty. The others never resented these attacks, these living sermons that his overpowering sense of duty and outraged feeling made him speak. They felt the power of his influence, and acknowledged his goodness, for it was full of charity. Even Guyon Vidocq resented not John Bar's corrections. He laughed, uttered another oath, and took himself away. But, alone, his face grew dark and angry, for he feared the power of John's goodness, and hated him.

My turn as hunter did not come until December 18, and my companion from the other house was an old acquaintance of mine in C—. We had been schoolmates and near neighbours when boys, but since that he had been away at sea. He was a quiet, amiable young man, and one of the steadiest in our camp.

Sometimes such an expedition kept the hunters away for the entire week, and sometimes they would get separated. In either case the night's shelter was a rough one, and dependent for safety and comfort upon the man's ingenuity and hardihood. But where two could keep together, both the labour and danger of those night camps in the snow were lessened. As game was killed, it was stowed away in what hunters call acache—that is, a hole for hiding and securing what we wished from the depredations of wolves and other wild animals; and then the ox-cart, when it was practicable—but generally, in winter, a sled drawn by hand—was sent out to bring in the game. My companion, Maine Mallory, and I started together up the frozen river; we agreed to keep together, if possible, and for that reason I carried a rifle and he a double-barrelled shotgun of large bore for throwing buckshot. We were dressed as warmly as our exercise would allow, and had, strapped on our backs, blankets and snow-shoes. Besides which, each one's wallet held five pounds of bread, pepper and salt, powder, shot, and bullets, and pipe and tobacco, not forgetting the most important of all, flint and steel. We proposed to follow up a branch of the Ottawa to a lake south-east of Mount K—, and there hunt with a party of very friendly Indians, who had a most comfortable camp in a spot near the lake. They were collecting winter skins to send down by us in the spring for sale in Montreal. Our first day's journey was about twenty miles on the hard frozen river, covered with a crust of snow so stiff as to render snow-shoes unnecessary; but it was hard work, for the weather was bitterly cold. We shot—that is, Maine Mallory did—a couple of partridges and a rabbit for our suppers, and halted early in a hemlock wood, where there was a northerly shelter of rocks; indeed, a crevice in the rocks was almost a cave for us, a cave where we gathered quantities of hemlock for bedding, and built at its entrance a huge fire, which, by night—when we had cut wood enough to last until morning, and had cooked and eaten our game—had made a deep hot bed of ashes. It was so cold, though, that we feared to sleep much; each took a turn at napping whilst the other fed the fire. The wood was as quiet as the grave; not a breath of wind; no night-bird nor prowling animal; nothing but the fine crackling of the cold. When I watched, I almost wished to see a wolf or bear—something to come in on the ghostly, silvered circle that the firelight illumined; something to start my congealing blood with a roar or spring. In the morning we took to the river course again, and went on, but resolved to try as hard as we could to reach the Indians' camp before another night. It was twenty-seven miles, we calculated, but we did it; and about nine o'clock heard the yelping of the Indian dogs that sounded our approach while we were yet half a mile from the camp. We knew the five Indians there; two came out to learn who drew near. Worn out and benumbed with cold, we gladly gave ourselves into their hands to be warmed and fed. They were well provided against severe cold, and soon made us comfortable; but we were too wearied the next day to do any hunting.

The Indians said the weather was growing colder every day, and the head-man, a middle-aged chief, called Ollabearqui, or Trick the Bear, told with an ominous grunt, that when the cold "grow bigger and bigger and the winds stay asleep, then Ollabearqui is afraid."

On the second morning of our stay among the Indians four of us went out after moose. Two, Mallory and an Indian, were to go around a mountain to the eastward, and Ollabearqui and I were to follow a valley which would bring us to the foot of the same mountain on the farther side, where we agreed to meet the others. A large, gaunt, savage-faced hound followed my Indian companion. He and I had each a rifle. We went quickly and silently through the white-clothed forests for about four miles. At length, where the small fall of the valley stream was held in great ice-shackles by the severe cold, and only a little pool of six inches diameter kept alive just beneath the icicles, we came out of the woods to a rocky, bushy foot and projection of the bare, stone-marked mountain. We had advanced to follow its base a short distance when my Indian companion, who had grown more careful and earnest lately, turned suddenly one side to a stiffly frozen covert of low bushes. The dog, before this most dull and dejected in his walk at his master's heels, now sprang ahead and into the bushes. In a moment he came out again with his nose close to the snow, and as he emerged raised his head and gave one short, fierce howl. Ollabearqui spoke to him in the Indian tongue, and the dog renewed his search, going back again to the little spring. The Indian at the same time pointed to the ground for me to see a track, but no mark of any kind was visible to my eye—not a scratch or impression on the hard snow-crust. Now the dog left the trees again and led us up the steep, rough side of the mountain —a most difficult path to climb, frozen as it was. One hundred and fifty feet or more up, the dog stopped before a mass of wildly piled rocks, and there barked loudly and angrily. We reached the spot, Ollabearqui some minutes before me, and discovered the narrow mouth of a cavern, at which the hound was furiously digging. The Indian cocked his rifle, saying, "Panther! Look out!" In a few moments the dog had made the hole big enough to admit his head and fore paws, and he attempted to crawl in, but at the same moment we heard a rumbling growl, like an infuriated cat's, but twenty times as strong, and the dog came out with a deep gash on the side of his head, cutting the mouth back a couple of inches. Again his master ordered him in. This time he entered entirely, and then we listened to the furious noises of the two beasts, in a desperate struggle evidently. In ten minutes the commotion ceased, but the hound did not return. I peered into the cavern, but could see nothing. As I rose to my feet after the attempt, I saw Ollabearqui, who had jumped to a point somewhat above the cavern's entrance, with his rifle at his shoulder. I looked where it pointed, and saw a tremendous panther-cat springing up the mountain-side—it had probably crawled out from some other opening of the cave. At the same moment I heard a report, and saw the beast roll forward on its breast, but as quick as a flash it rose again and dashed at the shooter. It was all done in a second, but I could see Ollabearqui trying to draw his knife. The panther struck him, and he lost his footing and rolled backwards from the ledge on which he stood; the panther saved itself from the fall, but bounded back, from the mere force of the spring, I suppose, to the other side of the rock. The savage beast was not more than twelve yards from me, but seemed to be unconscious of my presence. Stunned by the heavy fall, Ollabearqui did not rise, and I saw the panther crawl around the ledge to spring on his prostrate foe. I brought up my rifle, and took deliberate aim at the animal's shoulder. I fired. The panther made one tremendous leap, and fell with a dying yell on Ollabearqui's breast. I ran up, and, as I supposed, found the Indian only bruised and stunned by his tumble. As I removed the dead beast from his body, Ollabearqui grunted and uttered a laconic "Good!" He then rose somewhat lamely, and he and I set about digging at the cave. Soon we managed to pull out the dog, which was dead, and then, pushing the panther's corpse into the cavern, we stopped up both ends with heavy stones and went on, descending to a track through the forest again.

The luck was all mine that day, for when we had nearly reached the point where we were to meet our fellow-hunters, we heard, at a long distance beyond, a noise that the Maine hunter knows well—a dull, clacking noise, like the regular blows in a blacksmith's shop ever so far away. It was the trot of a moose. When at a slow pace they always strike their hoofs together in that way, as a horse overreaches. We drew behind some large trees, and, after ten minutes of anxious waiting, discerned a very large bull moose coming on a waddling trot towards us. He had probably been started by our companions, for he had his ears pointed back, and turned his neck every few minutes as if to catch some sound behind. He passed near Ollabearqui first, at about eighty yards. There was only a click! Ollabearqui's rifle had snapped. The moose, alarmed by the noise, increased his pace greatly, but came directly towards me, so that when I pulled trigger he was not farther off than twenty-five feet. He fell dead, a bullet right through his heart. My companion was not envious because of my good fortune. He scolded the erring rifle in his own language, and then said to me, "Good! good! You white-man very big shoot—ugh!" We joined Mallory and the other Indian soon after. They had only killed a fox. Together we made two sled-drags of the thickest, heaviest hemlock boughs, and loading the game—the panther-cat and fox on one sled, and the moose on the other—pulled them to the Indian camp.

The weather was too bitterly cold for hunting. Even the wild animals seemed not to go about any more than their wants required. So Mallory and I decided to buy some more meat from the Indians, and get them to go with us back to our lumbering station and help to carry the game on hand-sleds, which we could do with comparative ease on the river. The bargain was made, and Ollabearqui and two other Indians started with us the next morning, that we might reach our camp on the twenty-fourth, or on Christmas morning. No doubt the hope of getting whisky from our men induced the Indians to assent so readily to the proposition. The sled enabled us to take plenty of heavy furs and blankets for protection against the intense cold. Mallory and I also made a gallon of strong coffee before leaving the Indian camp; that we were able to heat three or four times a day, and would prove the greatest ally against the cold.

We made a long march the first day—nearly thirty miles—but suffered greatly from the unusually severe weather; and if our red friends had not taken us to an Indian mound to pass the night—which we used as a hut, packing all our furs against its stone sides and keeping up an immense fire in the centre, the smoke escaping where we removed a stone on the top—and had we not had the coffee to heat and drink continually, I really believe we should all have been frozen to death that terrible night. As it was, I remember it as the most painful and comfortless night I ever passed.

The morning came, and we could stir about; but the sun seemed to give no warmth, and a light wind was blowing to make the cold more searching. For some reason I could not explain to myself, I felt strangely anxious to get home. In the fitful naps I had caught during the night I had suffered from most painful dreams; but all I could remember of them were the faces of Guyon Vidocq and John Bar, and no sight of the camp or of the other men, only heaps of cinders where the log-houses stood. As soon as we had had our breakfast I urged my companions to get under way quickly. To my astonishment the Indians answered, "Us no go—us go back—so cold, ugh!—pipe of the Great Spirit gone out—us go back!" To our questionings and urgings they only grunted, shook their heads, and answered as before. So all Mallory and I could do was to let the fellows take their way. We packed the game in the stone mound, and piled stones and brushwood against its entrance and smoke-hole; and then with our guns, and the jug of what was left of the coffee on a sling between us, we started on our way.

That day's journey is a distressing remembrance. Despite the cold, we advanced briskly enough until noon. Then the wind grew stronger, whilst we got weak from the exposure. The cold increased. A numbness of mind and body was creeping over us, and our limbs were heavy to move. At about three we stopped, and in what shelter we could find, built a great fire; and heating the coffee as hot as we could swallow it, drank nearly all that remained, and ate a dinner. That strengthened and warmed us up enough to help us along until sunset. We were then only four or five miles from camp; but had not the wind gone down with the sun, we must have perished before reaching home, for from that time our sufferings increased, and both of us grew drowsy. Several times Mallory's halting steps stopped entirely, and he would have gone into the fatal sleep which precedes death from freezing, had I not shaken him and pushed and urged him. To me it was like walking in a sleep.

I dragged along almost unconsciously, and yet knowing enough to keep the river track and move my legs. The fact that Mallory was nearer death than I—which was shown by his constant attempts to lie down—kept me up. The sense of responsibility aroused my mind. I would implore him to try to walk for a little while longer, and then push him along again. About eight o'clock I got a fire going again, and made Mallory drink, the last drop. I told him we were not more than half a mile from the cabins—that he must rouse up now, and strive with me to reach our friends. "Was he willing to die," I asked, "just as we were on the threshold of safety?" The coffee helped him a little, but I had had none, so in that last struggle he was as strong as I. That half-mile was only accomplished after an hour's walking, and in every minute of that hour I felt that I could not make another effort.

At length we staggered to the door of Maine Mallory's cabin, and were saved! John Bar, who was in there, a refugee from the Christmas Eve frolic in our own cabin, rubbed my limbs, and poured cup after cup of strong coffee down my throat, and, when I was sufficiently recovered, gave me a good supper. The same was done for Mallory. But even in the cabin, with two immense fires and warm clothing, it was difficult to keep warm. The water in the drinking pail, four feet from the stove, was one mass of ice. Outside, that terrible night, the thermometer in Montreal, I heard afterwards, fell to 23 degrees below zero. With us there was no thermometer to mark the temperature, but it must have been lower.

Half of the gang of my log-house, including John Bar, were spending the evening where I had sought shelter, too wearied to go a hundred yards farther to my own quarters. The other five, one of whom was Guyon Vidocq, were having a regular drinking and gambling bout in the other cabin. We heard their yells from time to time. At about eleven o'clock John Bar left us to seek his bed. I doubted if he would find his bed very agreeable amid such an orgy as was reported to be going on under the other roof; so I, thoroughly enjoying the bright fire and new life after the exposure of the last few days, lingered a while longer, though utterly wearied, and answered the questions about our hunt. Maine Mallory had turned into bed long ago. But when my watch showed it was twelve, I got up to seek a night's sleep.

As I stepped into the intensely cold air, I was actually startled by the solemnity and beauty of the scene; for the moon had risen since my return to camp, and flooded the winter scene in the most glorious radiance. The gigantic trees were magnified in the pure, clear light, and their dark shadows stretched far on the glistening snow. Here and there were the fallen timbers mounded over by drifts. Beyond, the white mountains faded away to the pale sky. Not a sound, not a murmur of wind, not a voice to break the awful stillness.

With great thankfulness for my deliverance from the stark death that had been so near me all day, I looked up to heaven and remembered the blessed birth eighteen centuries ago when Jesus Christ came to the earth as a little babe.

Turning my steps to the other log-house, I wondered to see no light, and was surprised, too, that the riot there had ceased by midnight. As I walked the hundred yards, the song of the heavenly hosts of old sounded in my heart: "Glory to God in the highest, and on earth peace, good will toward men!"

Drawing near the cabin, I was amazed to see the door stretched wide open, and no light within. Instantly a dark foreboding fell upon me, and I remembered the fearful visions of the night before. What could it be that I was to encounter? I ran to the open door, and entered. No fire! only those few dull ashes. What did it mean? "Boys," I cried, "boys, where are you?" No reply. "Boys! Langdon! Vidocq! Bar!" and there came from near me a stifled answer, as if the speaker was but half awake. Trembling violently, I struck a match, and beheld John Bar, lying almost at my feet in a bundle of furs, and a pool of blood by him, and four other figures in everyday garments, without any other covering, stretched in different attitudes on the floor—sleeping, I thought. Yes, they were sleeping, but in death. Where they had fallen in drunken stupor the ice-breath of Death had stiffened them for his own.

"Is that you, Clare? Thank God! I am bleeding and freezing to death."

"Who harmed you, Bar? Tell me first—Vidocq? I thought so. In a second we'll help you."

Quicker than I can write it, I had run to the other cabin, aroused the inmates, and we had all reached the fatal cabin.

Some of us carefully removed Bar to the second house, whilst others chafed the bodies on the floor and poured warm drinks into their mouths to revive the spark of life, if it yet lingered. But they were frozen to death. The log-cabin in which my companions and I had lived for three months was now the lumberman's dead-house. There the four bodies were to rest until they could be moved to their graves. The next morning Guyon Vidocq's body was laid beside those of his companions. He had been found stretched dead on the riverbank.

Such was our Christmas.

It appeared that when John Bar had gone to his cabin he found four of the inmates lying drunk on the floor, the fires expiring, and Guyon Vidocq in a delirium of intoxication pulling everything to pieces—table, benches, etcetera —to pile them in the corner, and, then, as he said, light a real Christmas bonfire. John Bar immediately saw the danger that the poor creatures on the floor were in, and whilst he tried to get fires going in the stove and chimney-place as quickly as possible, he also exerted his influence to soothe Guyon Vidocq and make him cease his crazy work. But the presence of Bar seemed to madden Vidocq immediately. From the time the former entered the house, Vidocq cursed him with every vile oath his drunken lips could frame, and, when Bar attempted remonstrance and command, the infuriated maniac suddenly caught up a table knife, and plunged it in his opponent's side. Then with a yell Vidocq rushed from the house, leaving the door thrown back for the deadly cold to enter and complete his work. John Bar said that he fell when the knife struck him; that he had strength to crawl to a pile of furs and blankets; that he even tried to cover his companions, but could not; that he called for help as long as he had voice; and that, when I entered, an hour after the assault, he had lost all consciousness. The bleeding had ceased, but the sleep of the frozen was falling on him.

Those events of Christmas Day broke up the lumber-camp.

John Bar was not dangerously wounded, and when we were able to carry him on a sled to the nearest settlement he quickly recovered.

"And now, boys, you have had your stories, so let's off to bed. Captain Mugford, Ugly has gone to sleep over mine. He prefers sea narratives."

But Ugly heard his name, and broke off in the middle of a snore to come and put his paws apologetically on Mr Clare's knee.

The sail Harry and I had watched disappeared behind the point of rocks soon after Mr Clare commenced his story, and while waiting anxiously for her reappearance we listened with much interest to Mr Clare; and as he was finishing she came out again and stood to the south-west. Determined to investigate the mystery ourselves, we said nothing to the others. By the time we reached the deck to take our way homeward the little sail was hardly distinguishable. As no one noticed it, Harry and I went to bed, partners in a secret full of romance to us.

Chapter Seventeen.

An Exciting Discovery—The Cove wins a Name.

The next morning, at breakfast, Walter proposed that he and Harry Higginson should, after school, go down to the neck and shoot ducks, for Clump had reported that he had seen several flying over the cape. Our salt tute was at the table, and Harry, in reply, turned to him and said—

"Captain, won't you take my gun this afternoon and go with Walter in my place? Bob and I have a little secret service to attend to, which can't be postponed; so will you shoot the ducks for me?"

"No, Harry," the Captain replied, "I shall not think of shooting here, where we have the hunter of the Ottawa—the companion of Ollabearqui, the slayer of moose and panther-cats—ha! ha! Eh, Mr Clare?"

"Well, Captain Mugford, I will accept your kind offer, as I should like very much to have a few hours' shooting with Walter. I shall try it; but a fowling-piece and birds on the wing are different things from a rifle and running game as large as those I used to practise on, and I imagine that Walter will not commend me as the Indian did," was Mr Clare's answer.

After the morning lessons and dinner were over, Harry and I stole off together to make an investigation of last night's mystery. We took our way to the cove, which was soon to win a name. Although but three-quarters of a mile from our house, that part of the cape about the cove was the roughest and most inaccessible quarter in our possessions. I do not know that any of us ever climbed down to the water there before. The attractions in every other direction of fishing, bathing, shooting, and boating were so numerous that we had not carried our explorations in that direction. You may possibly remember there are places, sometimes within little more than a stone's-throw of your house, with which you never think of making acquaintance. Just such a place was the cove. It did not invite us particularly. It was not on the route of any of our pleasure expeditions, and, as I have said, there were points of interest in every other direction. But just above the cove was a high knob-shaped piece of grass and shrubs, dotted with many slabs of sharp stones that stood up like tombstones, and made the knoll look so much like a grave yard that we used to call it "our cemetery." There the sheep liked to feed just before night. It was a favourite spot, where they often came for their evening bite.

We crossed that, and commenced a scramble down a jagged, rocky declivity almost perpendicular. It reminded us of the cliffs in the islands of Orkney and Shetland, pictures of which, with the men suspended by ropes getting eggs from the nests that fill the crevices, have interested every boy in his geography book. With bruised hands and knees, and rather tattered trousers, we reached a ledge just above the high-tide mark. The cove was a perfect harbour. A boat there would be defended from every gale but a south-wester, and partly from that, whilst it would also be completely hidden unless from a boat right off the entrance of the cove, or unless some one peered over the dangerous cliff above; and what would one think of looking for in there? But we found enough to excite our astonishment. First there were a strand of rope and an oar on the narrow ledge, which we followed a couple of yards, and then saw an opening between two immense strata of stone. We looked in, and a ray of light that came through the fissure at the other extremity showed us a number of kegs, several bales of goods, sails, numerous coils of rope, and various other articles. We climbed in, and found also a rusty flintlock musket, standing between two barrels. If not as much frightened, we were as much astonished as Robinson Crusoe, when he discovered in the sand the print of a human foot.

As hastily as the difficulties would allow, we climbed up the rocks, and hurried towards the house, talking eagerly with each other while we ran as to what those kegs and bales might contain. Had they been hidden there by smugglers, or by whom? Were they now our property? What was to be the result?

Out of breath we reached the house, to find for our audience only Captain Mugford. He was reading in the sitting-room, and put down his book to hear our exciting revelation. When we had told him all, he asked us not to go to the cove again, until Mr Clare and he had had time to act on the information we had given, and told us to caution the other boys in the same way if we met them before he did. "And now," said he, "I will go out and meet Mr Clare and Walter—down on the neck, are they not? I have no doubt that the cave is the storehouse of smugglers."

"Smugglers!" we exclaimed.

"Yes," he answered, pulling on the pea-jacket that always came off in the house, and stowing his pipe in the breast-pocket. "Yes, smugglers, good-for-nothing scoundrels! who enjoy the good laws of the country, and all the advantages which a settled Government and established institutions give them, and yet play all sorts of tricks to avoid paying the required taxes to support that Government; while they do their best to prevent honest, straightforward-dealing traders from gaining a livelihood. Then, see to what an expense they put the country to keep up an army of coastguard men and a fleet of revenue vessels. There's the Hind sloop of war, with a crew of a hundred and twenty men, and some fifty cutters, large and small, with crews of from fifteen to forty men, on this south coast alone. If it wasn't for these idle rascals of smugglers, these men might be manning England's fleets, or navigating her merchantmen to bring back to her shores the wealth which makes her great and powerful. People talk of the Government paying for all this. Silly dolts that they are! It is not the Government pays; it is they who pay out of their own pockets; and when they encourage smugglers, which they too often do, they are just increasing the amount of their own taxes; and if they don't feel the increase much themselves, they are cheating their neighbours, though they have the impudence to call themselves honest men. I have no patience with those who encourage smugglers, and would transport every smuggler who is caught to Botany Bay, and still think the fate too good for him."

Having thus delivered himself, our worthy nautical instructor strode out to meet our fresh tute.

We took the news to Clump and Juno, who received it in mingled terror and amazement; and then we ran to find Drake and Alf, and pour it out to them.

Well, we had frequently heard about the doings of smugglers, but to have them burrowing on our cape, and be in a plot for their overthrow, were better than volumes of "Flying Dutchmen," "Pirates of the Gulf," "Gulliver's Travels," "Roderick Randoms," or even possibly of "Robinson Crusoes," and all other such made-up stories. Here they were fresh; we had watched their boat the night before; we had just come from their cave; and there was plenty ahead to imagine.

"Hurrah for our cape!" said Harry; "was there ever a jollier place for fun?"

Those days were palmy times for smugglers. High duties, in order to raise a revenue for carrying on the wars in which England had been engaged, had been placed on nearly all foreign articles. Wines, spirits, tobacco, silks, laces, ribbons, and indeed a vast number of other manufactures, were taxed more than cent per cent on their value, and some, if I recollect rightly, two or three hundred per cent. In fact, the high duties acted as an encouragement to smugglers, foreigners as well as Englishmen, and the whole coast swarmed with their luggers and other craft. Sometimes large armed cutters were employed, and their bold crews did not hesitate to defend themselves if attacked by revenue vessels, and sometimes came off the victors. The most disgraceful circumstance connected with these transactions was, that there were large mercantile houses in London who in some instances actually employed the smugglers, and in others gave them direct encouragement by receiving the silks and ribbons and laces, and other goods of that description, and disposing of them openly as if they had paid duty. Here, were men of wealth, and intelligence, and education, for the lust of gain inducing their fellow-men to commit a serious crime. They had relays of fleet horses, with light carts and wagons, running regularly to the coast, in which the smuggled goods were conveyed up to London. They bribed, when they could, the revenue men, and they had spies in every direction to give notice of the approach of those whom they could not bribe. They had lookout men on the watch for the approach of an expected smuggling vessel, and spots-men to select the best place on which she could run her cargo. They had also large parties on the beach, frequently strongly armed, to assist in landing the goods and to carry them up to the carts, or to the caves and other hiding-places, where they were stored when the carts were not in readiness. Every stratagem and other device was employed to draw the revenue men and military away from the spot where it was proposed to run a cargo. Sometimes a few goods, or bales of rubbish to look like goods, were landed in a particular spot, and allowed to fall into the hands of the coast guard, while the real cargo was being landed some miles away and rapidly conveyed up to London. When hard-pressed by a revenue vessel, if of a force too great to render fighting hopeless, the smuggling craft would throw the whole of her cargo overboard, so that when overtaken nothing contraband might be found in her. When the smugglers' cargo consisted of spirits, under such circumstances the casks, heavily weighted, were frequently, when in sight of land, dropped overboard, the landmarks on the shore being carefully taken. Thus the smuggler could return, when not watched, and regain her cargo. Sometimes the keen-eyed revenue officers had observed her proceedings when letting go the kegs, and on her return they could no longer be found. Sometimes the hard-pressed smuggler had not time to sink her cargo, and the kegs, still floating, were made prizes of by the cutter. At other times they were captured when on the point of being landed, or when actually landed, and it was on these occasions that the fiercest battles took place between the smugglers, aided by their numerous coadjutors on shore, and the revenue officers. If the lives of any of the revenue officers were lost during these encounters, the smugglers who were seen to have fired, when captured, were hung, while the less criminal in the eye of the law were transported, or imprisoned, or sent to serve on board men-of-war. It is scarcely too much to say that a large portion of the coast population of England was engaged in this illicit traffic. It bred also a great amount of ill-feeling between them and the coast guard, whom they endeavoured to mislead, annoy, and injure by every means in their power. Our worthy salt tutor had friends among the revenue officers, with whom he sided strongly; indeed, his natural good sense and right feeling would have prevented him from supporting a class of men who were so clearly acting against the laws of the country and all rules of right and justice.

Our tutors that evening held a consultation on board the brig, and decided that it was their duty to go over the next morning to inform the commander of the coast guard of the discovery Harry and I had made, and to let him take the steps which he might consider necessary. We two, of course, for the time became perfect heroes of romance, and could talk of nothing else during the evening but of smugglers and smuggling adventures. Captain Mugford possessed a large amount of lore on that subject, some of which he produced, much to our edification. He gave us an account of the fight between the Peggy smuggling lugger and the Bramble King's cutter. Three men were killed and five wounded on board the revenue cruiser, and a still greater number of smugglers lost their lives, though the lugger escaped on that occasion. She was, however, afterwards fallen in with by the very same cutter, when the smugglers showed fight at first; but so fiercely were they attacked by the brave commander of the cutter, that, their consciences making cowards of them, they yielded after a short struggle. It would have been difficult to convict the crew then on board of the murder of the cutter's people on the previous occasion, had not one of their number turned king's evidence. The captain and mate and two other men were accordingly hung, and the rest transported; but this summary mode of proceeding in no way put a stop to smuggling. The profits were too large, the temptations too great, to allow even the risk of being hung or transported to interfere with the traffic.

One story led to another, and at length our skipper came out with one which was voted, by general acclamation, to be superior to all the others. I cannot pretend to give it in old Mugford's language, so I present it in my own, keeping, however, closely to the facts he narrated. He called his tale:

"Jan Johnson, The Smuggler."

Some forty years ago, ay, more than that, I belonged for a few months to a revenue cruiser, on board which I volunteered, soon after my return from my second voyage, I think it was, or about that time. The cutter was stationed off this coast, and a hard life we had of it, for in those days the smuggling craft were large armed vessels, full of desperate men, who, when they could not outsail, more than once beat off the cruisers of the king. Among the most daring of his class was a fellow called Jan Johnson, though from having at different times many other names, it was difficult from them to determine to what nation he belonged; indeed, it was suspected that he was an Englishman born on this very coast, with every inch of which he was intimately acquainted.

He seemed to take absolute delight in setting at defiance all laws of God and man, and, among many other acts of atrocity, he was strongly suspected of the murder of a revenue officer. The officer had, it appears, been the means of taking a valuable cargo of goods belonging to Johnson, who some time after encountered him, when in discharge of his duty, near this place. It is supposed that the smuggler had attacked the unfortunate man, and, being by far the more powerful of the two, had grappled with him, and, plunging a long knife into his bosom, had thrown him over the cliffs. The next morning the body was discovered above high-water mark, with a knife known to belong to Johnson close to it, and on the top of the cliffs were seen the impressions of men's feet, as if engaged in a fierce struggle. A handkerchief, similar to one the smuggler had been observed to wear, was found in the dead man's grasp, and at a late hour of the night he had been met without one round his throat. A reward was therefore offered for his apprehension, but notwithstanding the sharp lookout we kept for his craft at sea, and the vigilance of the revenue people on shore, he had hitherto escaped capture.

He commanded at this time a large lugger, called the Polly, a fast-sailing boat, which could almost eat into the wind's eye, and when going free nothing could hope to come up with her; so that our only chance of capturing her was to jam her in with the shore, or to find ourselves near her in a calm, when we might get alongside her in our boats.

So daring was the smuggler that, though he well knew his life was at stake, he still continued to carry on his free trade with the coast, where he had many friends; yet, notwithstanding that his vessel was constantly seen, she was never approached except by those he trusted.

It was towards the end of October—I remember the time well—the days were growing shorter, and the night-watches darker and colder, when, after cruising up and down a week or so at sea, in hopes of falling in with a prize, it came on to blow very hard from the south-west. Our skipper was not a man to be frightened by a capful of wind, so, setting our storm sails, we stood off shore and faced the gale like men; for, do ye see, it is just such weather as this was that the smugglers choose to run across the channel, when they think no one will be on the lookout for them. Towards evening, however, it came on to blow harder than ever, so that at last we were obliged to up with the helm, and run for shelter into harbour; but just as we were keeping away, a sea struck the cutter, carried away our stern boat, and stove in one of our quarter boats. In this squall the wind seemed to have worn itself out, for before we made the land it suddenly fell, and by daylight a dead calm came on, followed by a dense fog. Our soundings told us that we were within a short distance of the coast, so that our eyes were busily employed in trying to get, through the mist, a sight of it, or of any strange sail which might be in the neighbourhood. At last, for an instant the fog lifted towards the north, like when the curtain of a theatre is drawn up, exposing close in with the land the white sails of a lugger, on which, as she rose and fell on the heavy swell remaining after the storm of the previous night, were now glancing the bright beams of the morning sun, exposing her thus more clearly to our view.

Before we could bring our glasses to bear, the fog again closed in, but every eye was turned in that direction to get another sight of her; we, doubtless, from our position, and the greater thickness of the mist round us, remaining hid from her view.

"What think you, Davis? which way shall we have the breeze when it does come?" asked our skipper of the old quartermaster, who was the oracle on such occasions.

"Why, sir, I should say, off the land; it looks clearer there away than it is out here."

As the old man delivered himself of this opinion, he turned his one open eye towards the point he indicated: for, though he had two orbs, and they were piercers, he never used more than one at a time—we youngsters used to suppose, to give each alternately a rest.

As he spoke, the fog once more opened a little.

"And, what do you say to yonder craft?" continued the skipper.

The old man's right eye surveyed her intently before he answered—

"I thought I knowed her, sir. As sure as we're alive she's the Polly, with Jan Johnson on board."

How he arrived at the latter conclusion we did not stop to consider. The words had an electric effect on board.

"You are right, Davis—you are right!" exclaimed our commander; then, in a tone of vexation, "And we have only one boat to chase her. If there comes a breeze, that fellow will sneak alongshore, and get out of our way. He calculated on being able to do so when he remained there, and no doubt has information that the revenue boats belonging to the station are sent off in other directions."

Every glass was now turned towards the direction where the smuggler was seen; for you must remember the mist quickly again hid her from us. Our skipper walked over to where the carpenter was employed in putting the boat to rights; but soon saw that there was a good day's work or more before she could be made to swim.

"It will never do to let that fellow—escape us!" he exclaimed briskly. "Mr Robertson," addressing his senior officer, a passed midshipman—an oldster in every sense of the word I then thought him,—"pipe the gig's crew away, with two extra hands, and let them all be fully armed. Do you take charge of the ship; and if a breeze gets up, press every stitch of canvas on her, and stand after the lugger. That fellow may give us some work; and I intend to go myself."

Having given these orders, he dived into his cabin, and quickly reappeared, with his cocked hat on and his sword by his side.

I belonged to the gig.

The boat was, as you may suppose, quickly ready. The order was given to shove off, and away we pulled, with hearty strokes, in the direction of the lugger. The fog for some time favoured our approach towards the spot where we guessed she was to be found, for we could no more see her than the people on board could us. Never, when roasting in the tropics under a burning sun, have I wished more earnestly for a breeze than we now did that the calm would continue till we could get alongside the long-looked-for craft. Not a word was spoken above a whisper, though we knew that the splash of our oars in the water would soon betray our approach to the sharpened ears of the smugglers, even before they could see us. We redoubled, therefore, our efforts to get alongside, when a light air coming off the land much thinned the intervening mist, showing us the Polly, with her largest canvas spread to catch the breeze, and now, as she loomed through the fog, appearing twice her real size, while her people clearly made us out. In a moment her sails were trimmed, her long sweeps were run out, and she was moving through the water, though not near so fast as we were pulling.

"Give way, my boys, give way," shouted our skipper, all necessity for silence being now removed. "Give way, and the lugger is ours."

With a hearty cheer the men bent to their oars and sent the boat flying through the calm blue water, casting aside the light sparkling foam which bubbled and hissed round her bows, as the story books about seagoing affairs say, such as you youngsters are so fond of reading. Well, the breeze freshened, however, before long, and we found that, though still decreasing our distance from the lugger, we were not gaining on her as fast as when she first made us out. We had, however, got within about a quarter of a mile of her, when we saw a man jump on the taffrail, and wave his hat at us as if in derision. Even at that distance, some of our people declared they recognised him as Jan Johnson, whom all of us knew well enough by sight. The next instant a skiff was launched from her decks, into which he jumped, and pulled as hard as he could towards the shore, to which he was already nearer than we were to him.

Here was a dilemma for our skipper. If we followed the outlaw, his lugger would very likely get away; and if we made chase after her, he would certainly escape, and she, probably, even if we came up with her, would not be condemned. The thought of the murdered man decided our commander, and in a moment the boat's head was turned towards the shore in chase of the skiff. Away we went, as fast as six ash oars in stout hands could send us through the water, while Johnson, still undaunted, continued his course; yet, in spite of his audacity, he well knew that it was with him a matter of life and death. It was indeed astonishing, when putting forth all his vast strength, how fast he sent along his light skiff; indeed, we gained but slightly on him in our six-oared galley, and we soon saw that he would reach the shore before we could overtake him.

"Give way, my lads, give way," shouted our skipper, though the men were straining every nerve to the utmost. "Give way, and we shall soon be up with him."

Talk of the excitement of a stag-hunt! it is tame in comparison with the interest men take in the chase of a fellow-creature. There is something of the nature of the bloodhound, I suspect, in our composition which delights in the pursuit of such noble game. A few minutes more decided the point, a cry of vexation escaping us as his boat touched the shore, and, coolly drawing her up on the strand, he was seen to make towards the woods.

"Shall I bring him down, sir?" asked the seaman who sat in the sternsheets with a musket, marine fashion, between his knees.

"No, no," was the answer. "We must take the fellow alive; he cannot escape us, if we put our best feet foremost."

Just as our boat's keel grated on the sand, Johnson disappeared among the rocks and trees, and we could hear a shout of derisive laughter ringing through the wood.

"After him, my boys, after him," shouted our skipper, as we all leaped on shore. "A five-pound note to the man who first gets hold of him."

And, except a youth who was left in charge of the boat, away we all went, helter-skelter, in the direction the outlaw had taken. He made, it appeared, straight inland, for we could hear his shouts ahead of us as we rushed on, hallooing to each other from among the trees. Not one of the party seemed inclined to get before the other—not so much that one was unwilling to deprive the other of the promised reward, but I suspect that no one was anxious to encounter Johnson singlehanded, well armed as of course he was, and desperate as we knew him to be. Our commander, being a stout man and short-winded, was soon left far behind, though, as he hurried on, puffing and blowing with the exertion he was using, his voice, as long as we could hear him, encouraged us in the pursuit. We had thus made good half a mile or more, when coming suddenly to the confines of the wood, or copse it might rather be called, a wide extent of open ground appeared before us, but not a trace of the fugitive could be perceived. Some of the foremost ran on to a spot of high ground near at hand, whence they could see in every direction, but not a figure was moving in the landscape. In the meantime our skipper came up, and ordered us to turn back and beat about the wood.

We had been thus fruitlessly engaged for some time, when we were recalled to the shore by a shout from one of our people, and, hastening down to the beach, we beheld, to our dismay, our own boat floating some way out in the bay, while Johnson, in his skiff, was pulling towards his lugger, now creeping alongshore out of the reach of the cutter, which still lay becalmed in the offing. What was most extraordinary, the lad who had been left in charge of the boat was nowhere to be seen, and, as far as we could make out, he was neither in her nor in Johnson's skiff. You may just picture to yourself our rage and disappointment; indeed, I thought, what from his exertions and excitement, our commander would have been beside himself with vexation. After we had stood for a moment, looking with blank astonishment at each other, he ordered us, in a sharp voice, some to run one way, some another, along the shore, in search of a boat by which we might get on board our galley, for she was too far off for anyone to attempt to swim to her. At last, some way on, we discovered, hauled up on the beach, a heavy fishing-boat, which with some work we managed to launch, and, by means of the bottom boards and a few pieces of plank we found in her, to paddle towards our gig. In our course, we picked up two of our oars which had been thrown overboard, and we were thus able to reach her sooner than we could otherwise have done. What could have become of our young shipmate? we asked each other; but not a conjecture could be offered. Johnson could not have carried him off; he would not have ventured to have injured him, and the lad was not likely to have deserted his post. At last we got alongside the gig, and on looking into her we saw Jim Bolton, our young shipmate, stretched along the thwarts, to which he was lashed. At first we thought he was dead; but a second glance showed us that a gag, made out of a thole-pin and a lump of oakum, had been put into his mouth. On being released it was some time before he could speak. He then told us that he was sitting quietly in the boat, when suddenly a man sprang on him with a force which knocked him over, and before he could collect his senses he found himself lashed to the thwarts with a lump in his mouth which prevented him crying out, and the boat moving away from the shore, and that was all he knew about the matter.

As Jim Bolton was very much hurt, we placed him in the fishing-boat with a midshipman who volunteered to look after him, and anchored her to await our return, while we with hearty goodwill pulled away in full chase of the smuggler. By this time, however, a fresh breeze had come off the land, which filled the sails of the lugger just as Johnson sprang from his boat upon her deck, and before a breath of air had reached the cutter he had run her far out of sight, winding his way among those reefs yonder. Seeing there was no chance of overtaking him in the gig, we pulled on board, and as soon as the uncertain air put the vessel through the water, we made chase in the direction we calculated the Pollywould take. For some time we cruised up and down over the ground where we thought we might fall in with her, but could see nothing of her, and we then returned to take out the midshipman and Jim, and to restore the boat to the fisherman.

We, with several other cruisers, were employed for some weeks in looking out for Johnson, but neither he nor the Polly was ever again heard of on this coast.

Ten years passed away, and I belonged to a brig in the West Indies, that clime of yellow fevers and sugar-canes. In those days the slave-trade flourished, for, as we had not become philanthropists, we did not interfere with those whose consciences did not prevent them from bartering for gold their own souls and the blood of their fellow-creatures. There was, however, a particular craft we were ordered to look after which had made herself amenable to the laws, having gone somewhat out of the usual line of trade, by committing several very atrocious acts of piracy. She was commanded, it was said, by an Englishman, a villain of no ordinary cast, who never intentionally left alive any of those he plundered to tell the tale of their wrongs. He sailed his vessel, a schooner carrying twelve guns, under Spanish colours, though of course he hoisted, on occasion, those of any other nation to suit his purpose. We all knew both him and his schooner, for before her real character was suspected, we had for some days laid alongside her at the Havanna, and were in consequence selected by the admiral to look out for her. We had been so employed for several weeks, when, one day towards noon, we made out a sail to the southward, towards which we ran down with a light northerly wind. As we neared her, which we rapidly did, we saw that she was a lofty ship—a merchantman evidently—and that she was not only not moving through the waters, but that her braces were loose, and her yards swinging about in every direction. Not a soul was looking over her bulwarks when we came within hail, but the men in the tops sang out that they could see several people lying about the decks either asleep or dead. We ran almost alongside, when I was ordered to board her with one of the gigs. Never shall I forget the scene which met my sight as I stepped on her decks; they were a complete shambles: a dozen or more men lay about in the after part of the ship, the blood yet oozing from deep gashes on their heads and shoulders, not one of them alive; while on the steps of the companion-ladder were two women, young and fair they appeared to have been, clasped in each other's arms, and both dead.

On descending below, we discovered an old lady and a venerable, old gentleman on the deck of the state cabin with the marks of pistol bullets in their foreheads, while at the door of an inner cabin lay a black servant with his head completely twisted round.

I will not mention all the sights of horror we encountered; the murderers seemed to have exerted their ingenuity in disfiguring their victims. There were several other dead people below, and at last, searching round the ship, we found stowed away in the forehold a seaman, who, though desperately wounded, still breathed. When brought on deck and a few drops of spirits were poured down his throat, he after some time came to himself, then told us that they had in the morning been attacked by a pirate, who, after they had made a desperate resistance, had carried them by boarding, when every soul in the ship was cut down or thrown into the sea except himself; that he, having fallen down the hatchway just before the pirates rushed on board, had stowed himself away amongst the cargo, and there after some time had fainted from loss of blood. While he lay there, he could hear the shrieks of his shipmates and the shouts and execrations of their butchers, he expecting, every instant, to share the fate of the rest. At last all was silent, the pirates made an ineffectual attempt to scuttle the ship, but were hurried off, probably, by seeing a sail which they mistook for us, or for some other cruiser.

Scarcely had the unfortunate fellow given this account, when the man at the mast-head of the brig hailed that there was a sail on the lee bow, and we were ordered forthwith to return on board. We all hoped that this might prove the pirate, for we were anxious to punish the miscreants. Taking, therefore, the wounded man with us—for being, thanks to the yellow fever, already short of hands, we were compelled to abandon the ship—we made sail in chase. For some time we carried a fresh breeze with us, while the stranger, which we soon made out to be a large topsail schooner, lay almost becalmed; but before we got her within range of our guns the wind also filled her sails, and away she went before it with every stitch of canvas they could pack on her. We also used every means of increasing our rate of sailing; but though our brig was reckoned a remarkably fast vessel, we found that, since we had both the same breeze, we had not in any way decreased our distance from her.

It was, however, a satisfaction to find that she did not outsail us before the wind, though there was every probability that, should she haul her wind, she would be able to do so; we therefore kept directly in her wake, to be ready to run down on her, on whichever tack she might haul up. At last, as the breeze freshened, we gained somewhat on her, when she hoisted Spanish colours: she had hitherto shown none, but this did not prevent us from trying the range of our bow-chasers on her, to bring her to. Several guns were fired without effect; at last a shot struck her main boom and severely wounded it. I never saw a better aim. After this, finding we lost ground by firing, we did not for another hour throw a single shot, nor had the schooner as yet returned our compliment, though she showed no inclination to heave to.

Away we bowled along before the breeze, throwing aside the now white-crested waves from our bows as we tore through the water. Every brace was stretched to the utmost, our spars bent and cracked, but not a sheet was slackened, though our captain kept his glance anxiously aloft to see how long he might let them bear the pressure. Again we overhauled her, and got her within range of our long guns, when a shot, directed more by chance, as the sea was running high, or, it might be said, a just Providence weary of the miscreants, than by skill, killed the man at the wheel, and lodged in the mainmast. Before another man could run to the helm the vessel yawed to port; the boom, already wounded, jibbed over and parted amidships, rendering the huge mainsail of no use, and creating much confusion on board. There was now no fear of her being able to haul her wind for some time, and coming up, hand over hand, with her, we ranged alongside.

If we had before any doubts of her real character, we had now none, for the Spanish ensign being hauled down, a black flag was hoisted at each masthead, and the accursed pirate was confessed. The outlaws, doubtless knowing that victory or death alone awaited them, showed their dark symbols in the hopes of intimidating our men, and made up their minds to fight it out to the last. At the same moment they let fly their whole broadside, which, though it did some damage, served to warm up the blood of our people, and made them return it with a hearty good will.

For half an hour or more, as we ran on, we thus continued exchanging broadsides, considerably thinning their crowded decks; but as some of our spars were wounded, our captain, fearing lest any being carried away, the enemy might escape, determined without delay to lay him on board, and to try the mettle of true men against their ruffian crew of desperadoes.

After receiving her broadside and pouring in ours, we put our helm to port, for she was, you must know, on our starboard side, when, running our bow anchor into her fore chains, our grappling irons were thrown, and we had her fast. With a loud cheer, our boarders sprang to the forecastle, and on to the rigging of the enemy.

Never shall I forget, if I was to live as long again as I have done, which is not very likely, the set of ferocious countenances which met our sight as we rushed on board. It was fearful work we were about, but our blood was up, and there was no quarter asked or given on either side. We did not stop to think. The pirates knew that there was no pardon for them, and seemed determined to sell their lives dearly. Our onset was too furious to be withstood, and in a minute we had cleared a small space on the schooner's decks abaft the foremast, but beyond that every foot was desperately disputed.

We had gained some ground forward, when, from the after part of the vessel, a determined band, led by the captain, pressed us hard. Twice we were driven back almost to our own ship, many of our men losing the number of their mess, but, finally, determined courage got the better of desperation. Inch by inch we drove the pirates aft—the chief of them, to do him justice, keeping always in the front rank, and I believe he killed, with his own hand, more of our people than did all his crew together, though he himself did not receive a scratch. During all this time the marines kept up a hot fire, pikes and pistols were used through the ports, and such guns as could be brought to bear were fired from each of the ships. I have seen plenty of hard fighting, and let me tell you, my boys, though it is very fine reading about, it is very dreadful in reality; yet never in my life have I gone through hotter work, on a small scale, than I did that day—the vessels, too, all the time rolling and pitching tremendously, and tearing away each other's rigging; indeed, it is surprising we did not both founder on the spot.

Well, we at last managed to clear the fore part of the schooner, by cutting down some and driving others of the pirates overboard, but fifty fellows still held the after part of the deck, uttering fearful oaths and execrations—they continued fighting on—when the deck lifted; fearful shrieks arose, a loud, dull sound was heard, and many of the pirates were hurled into the air, their mangled remains falling among us. For an instant every hand seemed paralysed, and we looked round to see what would happen next; but the explosion had been only partial, and during the confusion the remainder of the band making a rush forward, we again set to at the bloody work, and drove them back. A second attempt to fire the magazine was made, and failed. We were, by this time, secure of victory, though the remnant of the pirates refused to yield.

Their captain, whom I have spoken of, I now saw leap into the main rigging, when, waving his bloody sword above his head, he hurled it with the fiercest imprecations among us, severely wounding one of our people, and then, with a look of despair not to be forgotten, he plunged into the raging ocean, where a troop of sharks were ready to devour him. At that moment it struck me that I had seen his features in times long passed, and I found afterwards I was right.

When their leader was lost, the rest of the pirates submitted, and we had barely time to remove them, and to cut ourselves clear of the schooner, when, with the dying and dead on board, she went down; and on the spot where she had been, the hungry sharks were seen tearing their bodies in pieces, while the sea was tinged around with a ruddy hue. We afterwards fell in with the ship the pirates had attacked, for which we got a good round sum as salvage money, besides other substantial marks of the gratitude of the merchants in the West Indies, for having destroyed one of the greatest pests their trade had for a long time known.

The pirates were hung at Port Royal, in Jamaica, and the evening before their execution, one of them, for reasons I will some day tell you, desired to see me. I visited him in his cell, and from him I learned that the chief of their band, whose dreadful death I had witnessed, the man who had led them into crime and ruin, was, as I suspected, Jan Johnson, the smuggler.

The next morning Mr Clare and Captain Mugford went over to —, where they found Commander Treenail, to whom they gave all the information they possessed about the smugglers' cave. He heard this account with surprise, for he did not suppose it possible that any spot of ground had remained in that neighbourhood unvisited by his people. However, he was a man of action; and immediately that he comprehended the facts of the case, he signalled from his residence to a cutter which lay off in the bay to get under way, and to wait for him to come on board. "You will accompany me, gentlemen," he said to our tutors; "and as soon as we can get the lads on board who discovered the cave to show us its entrance, we will lose no time in routing out these smuggling vagabonds."

The old lieutenant commanding the cutter was waiting with his gig for Captain Treenail at the quay, and they, with our tutors, were quickly on board the Scout.

How proud Harry and I felt when the Scout's gig pulled up to the wreck, and we were summoned to show the way to the smugglers' cave. We jumped with alacrity into the gig, feeling as if we had the whole weight and responsibility on our shoulders of leading some important expedition. Captain Treenail received us very kindly, and cross-questioned us minutely as to the whereabouts of the cave and the various articles we had found within it. The cutter, when rounding the cape, had kept some distance from the little bay near which the cave lay, so that, even had smugglers been on the watch near it, they would probably not have been alarmed; the captain had hopes, therefore, that not only their goods but they themselves would be taken. To make the matter more sure, it was arranged that one party, led by Walter, who knew the cape as if he had been born on it, should go by land, accompanied by Mr Clare; while our salt tutor, with the rest of us, was to go in the cutter. Five seamen, with a petty officer, formed the land party, all well armed. They were to proceed cautiously across the downs, watching the movements of the cutter, and keeping themselves as much as possible under cover, so as not to be seen by any smugglers who might be on the lookout. As soon as the boat which took them on shore returned, the cutter's foresail was let draw, and with a fresh breeze she stood out of our cove. Our hearts beat quick as we glided rapidly on towards the scene of our proposed exploit. We might possibly soon be engaged in a scene of real fighting. There might be ten or perhaps even fifty smugglers concealed in the cave, with large stores of silks, and tobacco, and spirits; and if so, it was not likely that they would give in without striking some hard blows for their liberty. The breeze freshened, and our speed increased, though, as the wind was off the land, the water was smooth. Every inch of canvas the cutter could carry was clapped on her, that we might have the better chance of taking the smugglers by surprise. She heeled over to the breeze till her lee gunwale was under water, while we stood holding on to the weather rigging, and looking out for the entrance to the little cove. We neared it at last. Our hearts beat quicker than ever as we luffed up round a point which formed one of the sides of the little cove. Sail was rapidly shortened, the foresail hauled down, the jib-sheet let fly, and in half a minute we were at anchor. The next instant the crew, already fully armed and prepared, flew to the falls, and two boats were lowered, into which they and we, with Captain Treenail, the commander, and one of the mates of the cutter, and our own salt tutor, immediately jumped. Literally, before a minute had elapsed, two boats were pulling as fast as boats could pull for the shore. Harry and I now felt ourselves of more consequence than we had ever been in our lives before. We were expected to show the way to the cavern, and therefore, as soon as the boats touched the shore, we leaped out, and, pointing to the spot where the mouth of the cavern was to be found, ran towards it along the beach at full speed, followed by the officers and men, who might have had better sea legs, but certainly had not such good shore legs as we possessed. We were some little way ahead of the rest, and our object must have been very evident to any persons acquainted with the existence of the cavern. Just then the report of a firearm was heard, and a bullet whistled by us close to our ears. It did not stop us though, but made us dart on still more rapidly; and as we did so we saw a man climbing up the cliff above the cavern. Had any of the men with muskets been with us, they might have shot him. He turned round for an instant, and shook his fist at us; but before our companions came up he had disappeared. It took some time before the seamen who volunteered to go managed to climb up the slippery rock to the mouth of the cavern. When once two or three had gained a footing, they let down ropes, by which the rest easily got up. The forlorn hope, as the first party might be called, then dashed into the cavern, expecting, perhaps, to meet with a hot fire of musketry. Not a sound, however, was heard; no one appeared; on they boldly went. The smugglers might have had still more deadly intentions, and, it was possible, had prepared a mine to blow up anyone venturing into their cave. They were capable, according to our salt tutor's notion, of any atrocity. Still the forlorn hope went on without meeting with any impediment. More seamen entered, led by Captain Treenail, and others followed, till we were all inside; and torches being lit, the cavern was thoroughly examined. Not a human being was discovered, but the cave contained a far larger amount of bales of silks, and ribbons, and tobacco, and kegs of spirits, than we had supposed. It was, indeed, a far larger seizure than the coast guard on that station had ever before made. They were proportionably delighted, though they would have liked still more to have caught a dozen or two of smugglers, though not quite so valuable a prize as they would have been during the height of the war, when they would have been sent off to man our ships, and to fight the naval battles of old England.

When we found that no one was inside we told Captain Treenail of the man we had seen climbing up the cliff. He instantly ordered some of the most active young men of the cutter's crew to go in chase; but after hunting about for some time, they could find no possible way of getting up, and therefore had to abandon the attempt. The next thing was to convey the captured goods to the cutter. This occupied some time, as there were literally several boatloads of goods, to the value, I fancy, of a couple of thousand pounds. It must have been vexatious in the extreme, to any of the smugglers witnessing our proceedings, to see their property thus carried off before their eyes. It must have made them vow vengeance against those who captured it, and against us especially, who, they must have suspected, had given the information respecting the cave.

Among the articles found in the cavern was a rusty old musket. The old lieutenant, Mr Mophead, commanding the cutter, was a curiosity. I should like to describe him. He was very fat and very short, and very red-faced, which is not surprising, considering the hot suns which had shone on that face of his, and the vast amount of strong liquor which he had poured down his throat. Just as the last boatload had been got on board, Walter and his party appeared, not having seen any smugglers. Mr Mophead politely invited him on board. As soon as the boats were hoisted up, and the cutter was once more under way, standing from harbour, Mr Mophead took the musket in his hand, and, approaching Walter, said, with great form, "Mr Walter Tregellin, with Captain Treenail's leave—and I am sure that he will give me leave—I beg to present to you this weapon, that you may hand it to your respected father. He may like to possess it, to remind him how the cutter Scout, Lieutenant Mophead commander, was the means of relieving his property of a nest of smugglers, who would very soon, in my opinion, have taken possession of it."

Walter took the musket respectfully, though he could not help smiling; and our salt tutor blew his nose steadily for ten minutes. The same old musket my father afterwards gave to Harry and me, the discoverers of the smugglers' cave; and Harry relinquished all his rights in it to me.

It hangs now in my study, not far from the dog-collar—another memento of those good old times. We got back to our own cove in a very short time, and we landing, the cutter returned, with her valuable cargo, to her usual port. Clump, who had remained to take care of the house, informed us that he had been watching the downs above the cave, and that he had seen several men pass across the downs, and, running quickly, go towards the boat harbour often mentioned. They then jumped into a boat and pulled across the harbour to the village, where they disappeared. Such was the termination of the adventure for that day; but the romance, unfortunately for us, had not come to an end.

Chapter Eighteen.
October Sport—A Black Joke.

Only two weeks more! Letters had come from our parents to us and to our tutors, saying that we must return to Bristol on November the first.

Our great amusement at this time was shooting, as boating had become somewhat cold work. Now and then we knocked down a few straggling wild fowl, which at that early season had incautiously approached our cape, not aware of the sportsmen residing on it. Our tutors entered enthusiastically into the sport, borrowing guns from the town across the bay, and joining Walter and Harry every afternoon. We other fellows were also allowed to be there to take charge of Ugly, who entered into the sport as warmly as any of us. We generally stayed on the neck until near sunset, and just as the rabbits were out for their supper, started for home. That was Ugly's half-hour of sport, in which he was always sure to bring two or three rabbits round to the guns. Mr Clare could not shoot as well as Walter, or even Harry, at flying game, but he was first-rate at rabbits; let them jump as fast and high as they might, with Ugly only ten feet behind, and if our fresh tute pulled on them; they were sure to fall. With the Captain things went differently, much to our amusement; for our salt tute cared not how much we laughed at his failures, which all his shots were. He brought up his gun as if it were a harpoon, and always gave it a jerk, to help it shoot farther, when he pulled the trigger. The butt was seldom at his shoulder; and as he insisted upon putting immense loads in his gun, the results were sometimes disastrous to him and ridiculous to us. He often sprang back after a shot, as if he had been kicked by a horse, or wrung his hands, which had borne the recoil. His misses and misfortunes, however, never made him angry or dejected. After each failure, out came the red bandanna to wipe his brow, and as a shout of laughter greeted the performance, he would say calmly, with only a gleam of a smile, "So, boys, you think I missed, eh? Well, perhaps I did."

Clump and Juno having been much alarmed and excited by the discovery of the smugglers, we boys determined to profit by their disquieted state of mind, and hatched a scheme to afford some fun. We watched an opportunity to put it in execution. The time came one evening when our tutors did not return with us to the house after the afternoon's shooting, but went to the Clear the Track, to chat and settle some other matters until tea-time at seven.

Delighted with the arrangement, we boys ran to the house, and, getting up into our attic, began to make preparations for the trick we had concocted. There was nothing very original in our plan, I must own, nor was it, I confess, a very grand or noble thing to try and frighten a couple of poor ignorant negroes, for such was the object just then of our plans and preparations. Clump and Juno had a wholesome dread of smugglers and of the acts of vengeance of which they were supposed to be capable. We therefore arranged to dress up so as to make ourselves look as formidable as possible, and then to appear suddenly before the old couple. For this purpose we brought up from the wreck all the boat cloaks, greatcoats, and pieces of canvas which we could find, and sou'westers and tarpaulin hats, not forgetting some pistols and rusty swords. Besides these we laid in a store of pasteboard, and brown and coloured paper, and some laths, and string, and paint, and corks, and tow. With this abundant supply of materials we set to work to fabricate a variety of garments, such as we supposed smugglers would wear; at all events, such as were worn on the stage. We made a sufficient number of false noses to supply each of our faces, and long curling moustaches, which made those who wore them look very fierce. Some had wigs with wonderfully long shaggy hair, and others beards of prodigious growth. The greatcoats and cloaks served for most of the party, with belts round their waists stuck full of daggers made of wood, and a real pistol or two. Then we manufactured out of the canvas some high boots of huge proportions; the upper part capable of containing the whole of a man's personal luggage, and a day's supply of provender into the bargain. Nothing could exceed, either, the wild and ferocious appearance of our hats. Two of us wore black feathers in them, and two others were adorned with death's heads and cross bones: indeed, it must be confessed that we represented much more a band of pirates of two or three centuries back than a party of such smugglers as it was probable could be found on the British coast. Besides the real swords we possessed, we manufactured some hangers out of wood, which we hung by sashes at our sides. In fact, our disguises were complete in every respect, and so fierce did we all appear, that I truly believe, had one of us met another in any gloomy, half-lighted place, both heroes would have run away. Walter took an active part in all the arrangements, and being the tallest and well stuffed out, looked every inch of him a bold smuggler. It is wonderful what burnt cork and rouge and dark locks will effect in turning a mild, gentle-looking person into a fierce leader of outlaws. It was arranged that Drake and I should go down first before dressing up, to prepare the way for the rest of the actors, then he was first to step out, and I was to follow, and get ready. All being at length prepared, we descended to the kitchen, and strolled in there in a tired way, as if we were just in the humour to listen to the old blackies' talk and receive their petting. Clump, sitting bent over the fire to get light for his work, was cutting some tholes for the boat with his knife. "Hi," he said, as he saw us enter, "dat's good fur sore eyes."

And Juno, taking the pipe from her mouth, greeted us with a long whiff of smoke, and—

"I'se glad you'se cum—getten dark an glum 'ere, only ole Clump an me. What do yun Massas shoot?" Drake held up a couple of rabbits and three wild fowl. "Oh! de gorry—all dem!—well, dis chile nebber sees de like; an you'se gwine ter gib dem ter Clump agin—'spects so, all you'se don't want. De ole niggers be rich dis winter."

Clump, when he had got us seats, dusting the kitchen chairs with his long coat-tails, resumed his task, and as Juno's garrulousness ran on, he shook his head and chuckled, and muttered and grinned, just as if he were behind the scenes and prompting her to amuse us. He always had that funny way of grimacing and conversing with himself gaily, whilst Juno indulged in her talkative fits. He admired his old partner hugely. Once, when travelling with my father, he heard at an Assize some great lawyer make a speech, and said, when the orator had concluded—

"De'clar, Massa, dat's fine; dis nigger nebber hear anyone speak like dat afore, 'cept—'cept Juno."

By-and-by, as Juno's talk ran sluggishly, and the pipe required much picking and blowing, Clump got up to put by his work and light a lamp. But that we forbid, saying the firelight was so much pleasanter.

"Dat's so," said Juno, who had got her solace in good order again, and was all ready to start off on a new stream of jabber. "Dat's so—Clump not ole nuff ter know dat fire-lite more good dan lam-lite. Hi! hi! he only chile yit."

Drake interrupted there, to turn the conversation into another channel, by saying that we should leave the old house soon to go back to Bristol, and Clump asked, having taken a seat on the wood-box directly under the trap-door, "An you'se glad—glad? 'Spects de ole house git cole an dull to yous now; 'spects de yun Massas want git home?"

"Well, no, Clump," answered Drake; "I don't want to go away—that is, we would not want to go if—if—if we had not been somewhat frightened this evening."

Juno, because of her deafness, did not plainly hear what Drake had said, but she judged it in part from his manner and the assumed look of terror that he cast over his shoulder. So she bent forward anxiously, and asked him in a voice full of concern—

"Wat's dat, Massa Drake—wat's dat you say?" Drake drew nearer to her and repeated what he had said. "My hebbens, Massa Drake, wat did scar you?"

"Well, you see, Aunt Juno," replied Drake, looking cautiously about him again in the darkness of the room—"Bob and I were coming round at the back of the house, when we heard, or thought we heard, whispering, and on drawing nearer, we heard some fearful threats uttered; I cannot say what they were, they were so dreadful."

"Oh! don't talk so, Massa Drake, if dere was anybody, dey must be de smugglers, and dey will come to cut all our troats," exclaimed Juno, looking cautiously round over her shoulder.

I cannot say that even then, thoughtless as I was, I liked what Drake had said, because he had told a positive falsehood, and it was no excuse to declare that it was said in joke. Drake continued, his voice growing more and more tremulous every instant, as if with terror—"That's not all. As we crept away undiscovered, we heard the tramp of many feet coming up from the shore, and we shouldn't be surprised if at this very moment the house was surrounded by smugglers, come to carry us all off to foreign lands, to make slaves of us."

"Or to make soup of us," I cried out, wringing my hands. "Oh dear, oh dear, oh dear!"

"What has become of Walter and the rest, it is impossible to say," added Drake. "Too probably they have been already spirited away by the smugglers. Oh dear, oh dear, oh dear!" he exclaimed, and, jumping up, ran out as if to look for them.

Juno and Clump were, it seemed, very much alarmed, both rolling their large eyes round and round till they grew bigger and bigger. Certain noises outside increased the terror of the two poor souls, but I knew that they indicated impatience on the part of my companions. Accordingly, exclaiming that I would bear it no longer, I too jumped up, and ran after Drake. As neither of us returned, it was but natural that Juno and Clump should have supposed that we had been carried off by the smugglers. There the two poor souls sat, shivering and trembling with alarm, not daring to go out, for fear of finding their worst anticipations realised. At last, Clump—who was really a brave fellow at heart, though just then overtaken by a nervous fit—got up, and, taking his old gun from over the mantelpiece, prepared to load it. Several pair of sharp eyes had been watching proceedings from outside. Now was the moment for action. Led by Walter, in we rushed, and then advanced with threatening gestures towards the old couple. We were afraid of uttering any sound, lest the well-known tones of our voices should have betrayed us. Juno was at first the most alarmed. She did not scream or shriek, however, but, falling on her knees, appeared as if she was thus resolved to meet her death. Poor old Clump meantime stood gazing at us with an almost idiotic stare, till Walter, advancing, gave him a slap on the back, sufficient, it must be owned, to rouse him up. At first, the blow adding to his overwhelming terror, he rolled over, a mere bundle of blackness, into the wood-box, nothing being visible to us but two long quivering feet and five black fingers. But in a moment after, with his still unloaded gun in his hand, he sprang up like a madman, jumped over the table, and, not trying to open the door, burst through the window, smashing half a dozen panes of glass.

Who should open the door just then and come in, as Clump demolished the window and went out, but Captain Mugford! Having left Mr Clare enjoying a nap on a sofa in the brig, he had come up to the house, and, hearing the frightful noises in the kitchen, rushed in there. So much was he prepared by the yells that escaped for some tragic scene of scalding or other accident, that it required two or three minutes before he could take in the meaning of the commotion. But when he recognised in the fierce smugglers a party of his young friends, and when he beheld Juno's situation, and the shattered frame through which Clump had struggled, he took the joke, and broke into the most elephantine convulsions of laughter that I ever heard or witnessed. For half a minute, at least, he shook and shook internally, and then exploded. An explosion was no sooner finished than the internal spasm recommenced, and so he went on until I really feared he might injure himself. After five minutes of such attack, he managed to draw out his bandanna and cover his face with it, and then, whilst we watched his figure shaking and quivering, we heard, like groans, from beneath the handkerchief, "Oh ur–rh–ha—ar—uh! Bless me!" When he took down his handkerchief and happened to see Juno rising from her knees, he swelled up again like a balloon, and then eased off gradually in splutterings and moans as a dying porpoise. After which, he went and pacified Juno, and tried to explain to her what a wicked trick we had been guilty of, and that the band of smugglers, after all, were only the boys she knew so well, and he proceeded to disrobe us, one by one, so that the old woman might comprehend the joke. And so she did, but she sat motionless for a time, until some portion of her usual composure returned; and then she got up with many a sigh and mutterings of "Ki! ki! tink dat's wicked—frite ole Juno so—oh Lor!" but before tea was served, I heard her chuckling slyly, and turning towards us again and again as she poured the hot milk on the toast she was dishing up. We meantime were employed in peeling, and by degrees got restored to our usual appearance, and we then hurried up to our rooms to wash off the rouge and the marks of burnt cork with which our faces were covered. But the Captain sat down and shook quietly for a long while, the tears rolling down his face, and his fingers opening and closing convulsively on the handkerchief. And when tea was quite ready, he went off to hunt up Clump.

Mr Clare came in soon after, but we had, by that time, got the better of the fun, and removed all traces of the commotion. When the Captain joined us at the table, he had another laughing spasm before he could say or eat anything; but for the remainder of the evening he controlled himself pretty well, only breaking out about half a dozen times, and blowing his nose until it was very red and swollen. However, Mr Clare never heard of the way the poor negroes had been frightened by a practical joke, a thing he particularly disliked and had often spoken against.

Chapter Nineteen.
Last Days on the Cape—A Terrible Night.

And now, the time of our stay on the cape was drawing to a close. Only three days more remained, and they were to be occupied in collecting our books, packing trunks, and all the unpleasant little duties that become so tedious and dispiriting when, like a drop curtain, they announce the end of the play.

Perhaps if the days of our cape life had been prolonged, we should have regretted the detention from home, and yearned for our dear parents, looking on the cape, that had already lost some of its attractions, as soon to become a dreary point beaten by winter winds and seas and drifted across by the snow. But because we must go, therefore it was hard to go. What cannot be done, cannot be had, cannot be reached—that is just what the boy wants. As we could not yet actually realise the desolateness and barrenness of winter there, but only remember the delights and beauties of summer and autumn, we lost cheerfulness over the boxes and trunks, and sighed because of the brick walls, narrow streets, and toilsome school-work that were soon to bound our lives.

On a Wednesday we had been for our last afternoon's shooting on the moor. Our tutors had walked round to return their guns to the lenders over in the town. We strolled to the house through the fast fading afternoon light, talking of the memorable events in our half-year just closing.

"Now, I think," said Drake, "that our boat-race was the best fun of all."

"I don't," Alf answered, "though we had a good time then, I know; but what is there to compare with the cruise and shipwreck?—the excitement lasted so long and came out all right."

"Yes, it came out all right, but there was only a tight squeak that it did not go all wrong. I tell you what, fellows, I was horribly frightened that night, before we struck on Boatswain's Reef," said Harry.

Each of us but Walter added, "So was I."

"Walter, now you were frightened, too. Own now!" continued Harry.

"No, I was not, really!" answered Walter. "Somehow I never feel afraid on the water; and I think it must be because I was born at sea, you know, when our father and mother were returning from the West Indies. Now if I had been behind a pair of runaway horses, instead of aboard a good boat, I might have got shaky, I daresay."

"Well, my opinion is," said I, "that just the best time of all was finding the smugglers' cave; but I am afraid that, after we are gone, they may come down hard on Clump and Juno, and when we have—"

Walter interrupted me with "Nonsense, those fellows will know enough to keep hid or give the cape a wide berth after this. But talking about the good times we have had, I have enjoyed our shooting best of all, and so has Ugly, I'll bet—haven't you, Ugly?"

To which our bright little dog answered as well as he could by barking an assent, and jumping before us to wag his tail energetically.

"Hallo!" Harry exclaimed, stopping, as he spoke, to look off to sea; "there's a rakish-looking lugger—don't you see?—just there, to the south-east, near Bass Rocks. I wonder what she is after."

"After?" answered Drake, "why, probably running down to Penzance."

"I don't know about that," said Harry, who continued to watch the vessel with much interest; "it looks to me as if she were running close in, to anchor."

"Well, let her anchor if she likes. There's nothing strange in that, when there's not wind enough to fly a feather;" and after a few moments more, in which we resumed our way to the house, Drake continued—

"Haven't our tutors proved splendid fellows? I think the Captain is the finest old chap that I ever came across; and when Mr Clare is a clergyman I should like to go to his church—shouldn't feel a bit like going to sleep then."

To which we all gave a cordial assent, and, having reached the house, turned in there with the prospect of having some fun with Clump and Juno before our tutors should return. I stood at the door a few minutes. Sure enough Harry was right. Though it was too dark now to distinguish anything more than a hundred yards away, I heard the running out of a cable and then the lowering of the sails. "An odd place to anchor for the night," thought I, and so did Ugly, who was beside me, for he gave a low, uneasy howl.

Juno was laying the plates for tea, as I went in. After teasing her for awhile I joined the other boys. Soon Juno came out to the kitchen, and when she commenced to fry the hasty-pudding, we induced Clump to tell us some of his sea adventures, in the middle of which Ugly set up a furious barking, and a moment afterwards there came a heavy rap at the front door. It was the first time there had been a knock at a door of our old house since we had been in it.

Clump, leaving his story unfinished, took a candle, and Drake and I followed him into the dining-room, which he had to cross to get to the front door. But by the time we had entered the dining-room a stranger had walked into the hall, and had also proceeded to open the door opposite us. Ugly, who was greatly incensed, jumped forward and took hold of a leg of the stranger's trousers.

Our visitor was a small, rough, ugly man, with a terrible squint in his eyes and a voice as unpleasant as his face. He had no collar, only a handkerchief about his neck, and wore a large, shaggy flushing jacket. His first act was to kick Ugly halfway across the room, with the salutation: "Take that, you damned cur, for your manners, damn you!"

Ugly made at him again fiercer than ever, but I caught him in time and held him.

"Wat will you 'ab, sir?" asked Clump in a dignified voice.

"What will I have, ay? I'll have that cur's life if he comes at me agin, and I want to know, old nigger, if,"—here the rough customer spit some tobacco-juice on the floor—"I want to know if you kin 'commodate four or five gents for the night, ay?"

All of Clump's spirit was aroused, and he stammered as he replied—

"No, mon; n–o–o–o! We dussen keeps no ho–o–o—hotel 'ere, we dussen. You'se find tabben ober end de town. Dis am Massa Tre–gel—Tre–gel—Massa Tregellin's privet mansion."

"Ho! ho!" answered the man, slapping his hat down on his head and spitting again. "Massa Tregellin's house, is it? Look here, boys, you just tell your dad, when you see him, that he has got a foolish, consequential nigger and a mean, tumbledown affair of a hut, if it can't 'commodate some poor sailors. Howsumever, I'll go back to my lugger, and bad luck to your mansion! Old nig, look 'er here—perhaps we'll see each other again." He looked slowly all round the room, and went out, slamming the doors after him.

Fifteen minutes afterwards our tutors came in, and when they heard of our visitor Captain Mugford waxed wroth.

"I wish I had been here," he exclaimed; "if I wouldn't have put that scoundrel off soundings in about half a splice! The impudent fellow, to attempt to lord it in that style in a gentleman's house. What do you think of it, Mr Clare, eh?"

"Oh, not much, Captain Mugford. The man was probably tipsy, and was of course a bully, or he would never have talked so before boys and a poor old negro. I am glad neither Walter nor Harry was in the room."

"So am I, sir," said Walter; "we were in the kitchen and came in when we heard the loud talking, just as the man slammed the doors in going out. We could have done nothing more than order him out."

After tea we boys went into the kitchen again, leaving our tutors playing at chess, which Mr Clare was trying to teach Captain Mugford. That kitchen was a favourite resort of ours in the evenings, and Clump and Juno liked to have us there. There was a famous fire—three or four fresh logs singing over a red mass of coal; plenty of ashes; and a whistled tune with a jet of smoke right from the heart of each stick. The brass fire-dogs were extra bright, reflecting the blaze on all sides. Some chestnuts and potatoes were roasting in the ashes, and Clump had provided some cider to treat us to, this last night of ours on the cape. So we pulled our chairs close around the fire, Clump sitting at one end, almost inside the chimney-place, smoking his pipe, and Juno at the other end, also almost inside the chimney-place, and smoking, too, her pipe. Hi! How they grinned, and chatted, and smoked. After awhile, when we had had a full hour of real fun, quizzing the old folks, telling stories, eating chestnuts and potatoes, drinking cider, and listening to stories of the West Indies, Walter and

Harry got up to clean their guns.

"Wen you'se cum 'ere nudder time, 'spect dese ole black folks be gwine 'way—be gwine 'crost de ribber Jordan?"—exclaimed Juno, with a long sigh.

"Now, don't talk in that way," said Harry; "why, marm Juno, you and Clump will live to dance at my wedding; see if you don't; and now, Juno, just give us a kettle of hot water, will you, to rinse out these gun-barrels with."

When the guns were washed, dried, and rubbed off with oil, I said to Clump, "Have you got any bullets or buckshot?"

"Don't know, Massa Bob—'spects so, en my ole tool-box."

"Why," asked Drake, "what are you going to do, Bob, with bullets and buckshot?"

Clump was down on his knees in the closet, overhauling the tool-box he had spoken of.

"Well, Drake, I'll tell you if Clump finds the articles," I answered.

"Have you got any, Clump?"

"Yah, Massa, 'ere's a han'ful."

"These bullets and buckshot," I continued, "are for Walter and Harry to load their guns with; for, just as sure as that fellow came here this afternoon, just so sure, I believe, he will be back here before morning with more like him."

"What stuff," sang out Walter, laughing; "what puts that in your head, Bob?"

"I don't know exactly what, Walter, but I suspect it, and I have not liked to say anything about it before, because I was afraid of being laughed at. But the more I think of it, the more certain I am that the man who was here to-night is one of the band of smugglers who owned the goods taken through our means by the revenue men. There are others with him, and, mark my word, they have not come back for nothing. Now do, fellows, load your guns. We needn't say anything and get laughed at, for the Captain will surely laugh if we tell him my suspicions. You can take your guns upstairs, and then, if anything does happen before morning, you'll be all ready."

"Well, Walter," said Harry, "suppose we do—it's good fun at any rate to make believe that robbers, and outlaws, and smugglers, and all other sorts of odd visitors are coming—and—I cannot help owning that what Bob says sounds probable. So here go two bullets for this barrel, and nine buckshot for the other. Come, Walt, load up! Don't you shake in your boots already? ugh!"

"It is curious that we should have pretended to be smugglers if smugglers really do come. Probably that makes Bob fancy they will come; still, I wish that we had not frightened the old people so," said Walter, loading his gun; and a few minutes later Mr Clare opened the kitchen door and called us in to evening prayers. As they always did, Clump and Juno assembled with us in the dining-room.

There was something very impressive in those few moments before the chapter for reading was found. There was the sound of the turning over of the Bible leaves, and that of a light, pattering autumn rain without, (it had commenced after dark), besides the comfortable crackling of the wood-fire, and the occasional snapping of the fresh logs. The old, devoted, pious negroes; the rugged, benevolent Captain, with an expression of thought and reverent waiting in his face; and we boys, so full of youth and spirits, sat thinking—soberly, and perhaps solemnly—how neither sickness nor harm had come near us; what blessings of pleasure, health, and strength had waited on us all during half a year; how those dear ones separated from us had been preserved from suffering and calamity, and were hoping to meet us before another week had commenced; how the common ties and associations that had united us so happily and so long were soon to be sundered. Those and many other—some graver, some lighter—thoughts, in those few seconds, occupied our minds, whilst Mr Clare turned over the leaves beneath the table lamp, and then his clear, strong voice slowly and feelingly uttered the words: "I will say of the Lord, He is my refuge and my fortress: my God; in Him will I trust. Surely He shall deliver thee from the snare of the fowler, and from the noisome pestilence. He shall cover thee with His feathers, and under His wings shalt thou trust: His truth shall be thy shield and buckler. Thou shalt not be afraid for the terror by night; nor for the arrow that flieth by day; nor for the pestilence that walketh in darkness; nor for the destruction that wasteth at noonday... Because thou hast made the Lord which is my refuge, even the Most High, thy habitation... For He shall give His angels charge over thee, to keep thee in all thy ways. They shall bear thee up in their hands, lest thou dash thy foot against a stone... He shall call upon Me, and I will answer him. I will be with him in trouble: I will deliver him and honour him. With long life will I satisfy him, and show him My salvation."

And when the prayers had ended, we separated quietly for our beds, the Captain going off as usual to the brig.

I turned the key in the hall-door as he went out—the first time such a thing had been done during our stay on the cape. Ugly coiled himself up on the horsehair sofa in the dining-room, and in half an hour more, I suppose, every soul in the old house was asleep.

I dreamed that a lot of rabbits were in a hole together and making a humming noise, which, I believed, was a whispering they were having together, and I wanted to hear what they said, but that Ugly made such a barking I could not. I woke up, and, sure enough, Ugly was very noisy in the room below, barking regularly and harshly. No one else in the house seemed to be disturbed. There was a placid snoring in the attic, a pattering of rain on the roof, and a splashing of water, as it ran off steadily in a stream to the ground. But in a minute or two, between Ugly's barks I thought I heard something which recalled what I had been dreaming of, the rabbits whispering in their burrow. I listened. Yes, some persons outside the house were talking together in low voices. I crawled to a window and looked out. There was an indistinct group of three or four persons standing by the rock, twenty yards from the house. Their talk was only a murmur of different voices in discussion, sometimes louder, sometimes fainter; but as I watched, one of the group struck a light, and I saw in the flash four or five or more figures, and the face of the man who had entered the house in the evening, who was now holding a lantern to be lighted, and was also looking up at the house. It was a dark lantern, I suppose, for the light was shut up in some way after that. I shook each of the boys and told them to look out of the window, and then I ran into Mr Clare's room and woke him. When he saw that some sort of robbery or attack was to be made on the house, he exclaimed, "I hope they do not know that the Captain is alone in the brig," and ran downstairs to bolt all the doors and windows as securely as they could be fastened, and awaken Clump and Juno, who slept in a little room off the kitchen. Not a lamp was lighted in the house, but the smugglers had heard the noises made, and now, talking and swearing aloud, approached the door and turned the handle. Being bolted within, they could not open it.

"Hullo! hullo! I say, you Tregellin fellows, wake up!"—it was the voice we had heard before—"wake up and let us in?"—it sounded as if he turned to his companions then, and laughed and muttered something—"here's some decent sailor-boys as wants a drop and a bite, so wake up quick, boys and niggers!—let us in, I say, or we'll break open the doors, and break your bones into the bargain."

At the conclusion of the speech, they all beat on the door and house with fists and sticks, and laughed loudly at their leader's joke. Mr Clare now went down the narrow, creaking stairs again to the big door they were pounding against so fiercely, and from behind its defence answered the summons.

"Men: this is a private house, and you must go away. You will get nothing here, and we are armed."

"Hurrah!" they answered without. I shall omit the terrible oaths with which they loaded every breath they spoke. "Who are you, big voice?"

"No matter," called out Mr Clare, "who I am. I suspect who you are, and we do not intend to let you get in here—that is all."

"That's a lie—we'll be in in ten minutes and make your bass a squeak. If you don't open this 'ere door in a jiffy—we'll make grease-pots of you along with them niggers. Look what we'll do with your castle—just what we have been doing with the old hulk down there on the rocks."

As he spoke, the darkness in the house withdrew to the holes and corners, and flashes of red and white light shot into every window and played on the walls, reflected from the midnight sky that had suddenly kindled to a blaze. The outlaws had set the old wreck on fire—our dear old school-house.

Could the Captain be there, sleeping yet? or had they killed him?

Ah! that doubt about Captain Mugford's safety magnified the danger of our own situation to our imaginations. If those outlaws could burn, in madness, such a harmless thing as the castaway brig, and could conquer such a powerful man as our salt tute, what might they not do here to us?

The hour—the yelling and swearing and banging at the doors—the lurid glare flashing from the sky to show us each other's fear-stamped countenances—those united to bewilder and appal us boys at least.

Juno, too, was upstairs in our room, sitting on a low chair, perfectly silent, but overcome by dread. But Clump, who now showed the courage he really possessed, was active with Mr Clare downstairs, strengthening every window and door. He was not afraid. His old spirit was aroused, and, in the defence of his dear master's children, he was anxious to prove his courage and fidelity.

"Harry," Mr Clare called up the stairs, "bring me your gun. I shall want that down here. You say it is all loaded and ready, eh? Well, bring it down. Walter, you keep yours upstairs, and all you boys remain there until it is necessary to come down; and now, Walter, don't fire unless there is absolute necessity. The rascals can't burn this house unless they light the roof, and they can't stay here all night to do that, for the light of the Clear the Track will bring over some of the townspeople. Poor Mugford! poor Mugford! Bob, you climb up to that little window in the south gable-end, and see if you can detect any movement about the wreck."

Harry handed him the gun, and I climbed to the lookout, relinquishing Ugly, whom I had been holding, to Juno's care. He had been ordered not to bark, so now he only panted fiercely and listened intently.

The smugglers, after vain attempts at the front door—they could have smashed in the windows, shutters, latches, glass, and all, but their small size and height from the ground made them most dangerous to enter by when there were defenders within went round to the back of the house, and presently I heard a great ripping and banging of boards there, and Mr Clare's voice call quickly—

"If one inch of you enter there, I will fire—understand that."

Then we heard a shot, but knew by the report that it was not Harry's gun, and Drake called down the stairs, "Clump, who fired?"

"De smugglers, Massa; one den shoot tru de winder at Massa Clare, but tank de Lor, the scoundrel miss."

Just then I saw—and how the blood coursed with one cold sweep from my heart and back again—amid the hot flames of the burning wreck, Captain Mugford's figure. He sprang from the deck to the rocks and was rushing towards the house. I turned and called the good news, but found that Juno and I were alone. The others, too much excited and interested in the contest to remain longer prisoners in the attic, had got on the stairway, and when I looked down on them Walter was on the bottom step with his gun cocked.

Now many steps and the yelled-out blasphemy of the smugglers came round the house again to the front. Though, as we knew afterwards, two remained to keep Mr Clare occupied there, whilst the three others were to try the windows again.

Captain Mugford must be near. Oh! that he could get here safely. Ugly jumped by me, and, uttering a savage bark, sprang downstairs and past Walter. He had escaped from Juno's charge. As he flew about the rooms downstairs, a whole sash and shutter in the south-east room were driven in by a blow of an immense beam, and in another second half the body of a smuggler was above the window-sill. But with a tremendous leap Ugly reached him and pinned him by the throat. They tumbled back together. Then we heard a new voice—Captain Mugford's!

"You cowards, you hang-dogs, you scum of the sea, you dark-hearted blackguards—take that! Aye, villains!—and that!"

Two pistol shots were heard. Harry jumped to open the door for Captain Mugford. Walter stood ready beside him with the gun. I ran with Drake to the open window, to see if harm had come to our dear salt tute, and Alfred had hurried in to where Mr Clare was alone guarding the back-door and broken windows, for he had sent Clump, not knowing of our being downstairs and of the Captain's coming, to fight where we were. Clump had a short iron bar in his hands. I saw the man whom Ugly had gripped fallen on his knees and cutting our gallant little dog from his neck with a knife. One outlaw was stretched on the ground. Another was struggling with the Captain. He was a large, powerful fellow, and seemed to be getting the better of our now much-exhausted tutor. As I looked, the prostrate man rose, and both he and the one whom poor Ugly—now dead on the grass—had attacked came to help crush the Captain. Then the front door was flung open. Walter fired, and the man who had killed our brave dog dropped the knife he held, and, clasping his left shoulder with his right hand, screamed out a terrible oath, and, yelling with pain, ran from the struggle. At the same moment—all these events, from the time Captain Mugford arrived until the door was opened to admit him, not occupying probably three minutes—the Captain fell beneath his adversary, whose fingers clutched his throat, and the infuriated outlaw seemed determined to finish him. Walter could not fire again without shooting the very one for whose safety alone he would fire. But Clump jumped out with his iron bar and struck the assailant on the head. The Captain was released just as I saw the other miscreant level a pistol at Clump. I called, "Oh, Clump, Clump, take care!" With the sound of my voice came the sharp, fatal crack of the pistol, and Clump fell back—dead!

Two minutes more and all the smugglers were in full flight. The old, grey-headed, faithful, true-hearted Clump was dead, and Juno stretched unconscious on her husband's body. Ugly, all hacked to pieces, lay in a pool of blood, yet gasping. Captain Mugford, wounded, bruised, and exhausted, sat on the doorstep. Mr Clare was leaning over Clump with a hand on the pulseless heart. The burning wreck yet lighted the heavens, and the horrid scene at the very doorstep of our home of such a happy half-year.

Chapter Twenty.
A Retrospect and Farewell.

It is fifty years ago and some months since that rainy, bloody, flame-lit October night. And now this cold, wintery, blustering midnight, I—the Bob Tregellin of my story—sit writing this concluding chapter.

There is a coal-fire glowing hot in the grate. There are shelves and shelves of books; easy-chairs sprawling their indolent figures here and there; a curled-up bunch of fur purring in one; an old black setter-dog dreaming—as I can see by the whine in his quick breathing and the kicking of his outstretched legs—on a bearskin rug before the fire; and a circle of bright light from a well-shaded lamp falls about my table. Yes—but I shall get up now for a minute and take down the old musket and dog-collar, the sight of which always vividly recalls those happiest months of my life—Fifty Years Ago.

As I replace them the storm without comes in a heavier, fiercer gust. I hear it rush in a whirl up the street. I see it almost lift the heavy curtains over the window, as if it would come in and rest itself. I hear it whistling through all the cracks and keyholes of the house—whistling dismally. Its voices, and the rumbling of a hack in some neighbouring street, remind me of storms I have heard, lying comfortably in my snug attic bed in the old house on the cape—the wind and the waves dashing up the rocky shore.

That strong whiff disturbed pussy's and "the Captain's" (so I have called my old setter friend) nap, for puss stands up on her morocco bed and arches her back like a horseshoe, and then springs, with a jolted-out "mew–r–r–r," right on my table, and proceeds to walk over this manuscript, carrying her tail up as if she wanted to light it by the gas and beg me then to touch it to my pipe and stop scribbling. So I shall presently. And the Captain strolls up to lay his cold nose on my knee, slowly wag his silky tail, and look kindly into my face with those soft, big eyes, as if he would say, "Come, master, don't be low-spirited."

You are right, old fellow! I was somewhat sad about leaving the pleasant companionship I have held through my pen with brothers and friends of the old time, and a goodly number of those who are young now, while I am so no longer, except in memory and heart. Youth has come back with these pages, and perhaps you are tired with me, but I—I shall never tire of the young—the glorious companionship of the pure, merry, brave hearts that look undaunted and without suspicion on the great road stretching far into the Future, and fading only to reappear in mirages of splendour in a brilliant sky.

There! I have smoked my pipe: and now, Miss Puss, stretch yourself in the chair again, and you, Captain, resume that dream by the fire. I have got a few more lines to write before my invisible friends leave me.

From that autumn night, 1830, to this winter night of 1872, no clue has ever been discovered to the murderers of faithful old Clump. About Christmas time of the same year Juno closed her earthly eyes in the old Cape House—to open them again, I fervently believe, in heaven.

Mr Clare lives—a venerable clergyman in one of our great cities—his head and heart yet labouring earnestly in the Great Cause he serves.

Captain Mugford sleeps in the home of his adoption—the ocean. Five years after our six months together he sailed from Bristol as boatswain of a splendid ship for the Pacific. A fortnight after, he was spoken by a homeward-bound brig, and that was the last ever heard of honest Roland Mugford, or the ship he sailed in. I hope seas, winds, and undercurrents, however rough they may have been, left undisturbed the red bandanna and the short black pipe. And we feel sure that the mother's prayers were answered, and that the boy who ran away from her in his youth came back to her,—whither her memory was a beacon light—the Eternal Harbour, unstirred by storms.

Walter is a man of eminence—a diplomatist—and Harry a merchant, a cheerful, generous-hearted man, whose name is the synonym of honour, and whose hands "to do good, and to distribute, forget not."

Drake, who entered the army after travelling in every strange and dim corner of the globe—frozen up in the Arctic Seas, perspiring in the interior of Africa, exploring among the western wilds of the Rocky Mountains, and doing other things adventurous in every out-of-the-way part—finally went with all his honest, hot zeal to India, where, fighting his country's battles, he spent many years of his life, and came back a general and one-legged man. Now he stumps about in this same library, but manages to take me travelling thousands of never-weary miles; and many and many a time do we walk, and shoot, and swim, and race, and fight over and over again that happy time at the cape.

Poor Alfred—the best of all of us—died before his thirtieth year, nursed by a few devoted Africans, at his missionary station in the southern Atlantic.

And I, whom the general calls "Vieux Moustache," have finished an old Boy's Story of "Our Salt and Fresh Water Tutors."

The End.